The Model's Last Pose

The Pearl Hotel Cozy Mystery Series

Book 1

NANCY PENNICK

The Pearl Hotel Mystery Series is dedicated to my sister, Susan, who encouraged me to bring Serena to life. To my cousin, Beth, who always says yes when I ask for help. And, to my husband, Ron, who reads every word I write.

Chapter One

"I have writer's block!" Serena dropped her forehead onto one arm as she pounded the table with her fist. "My publisher is hounding me for the next book, and I have no concrete ideas. No decent plots. Nothing," she moaned.

"You're overwhelmed, Serena," her friend Mia said, patting her arm. "Your first book was wonderful, a best seller, and you're afraid the next one won't live up to its success. Take a few deep breaths. I've ordered some tea."

Serena peeked through her fingers. "Oolong?"

"Yes."

"Did you get those little almond cookies I like?"

"Of course."

"What would I do without you?" Serena lifted herself into a sitting position. "If it wasn't for you and this hotel, I wouldn't have completed the book, let alone write it."

"Not true. You had the story in you the whole time, just waiting to burst onto the page." Mia smiled.

"You are a sweetheart, my friend, but you know you're lying." Serena pointed at Mia. "I based the book on a true story. *Your* story. Some sort of magical entity intervened on the day we met. Perhaps it was fate." She smiled. "An exceptional black woman, me, who'd just turned forty, meets an outstanding Japanese woman, you, who planned to marry the love of her life. However, you only revealed a small amount of an unbelievable, incredible account of your life that day."

"Quite true, and I agree with you about fate. Any rideshare driver could have picked me up that day, but it was you."

"We found each other in the most unconventional way and developed a friendship," Serena answered, cocking her head to one side. "How old are you, Mia?" She raised a brow. "Have you even turned thirty?"

"I did." Mia nodded. "I also celebrated my first-year wedding anniversary."

"My, how time flies."

Serena recalled the day Mia hopped into her car, her silky black locks flowing in the breeze. "Where to?" Serena had asked, noticing the woman's beautiful chocolate eyes. An observer of people, she'd also seen something else. Fear with a spark of determination.

"Golden Gate Park, please."

Sweet. Polite. "Sure." Serena engaged in light conversation during the drive, but her passenger remained mostly silent.

When Mia asked her to wait in the lot, Serena instantly agreed. She always carried a notebook to scribble down her thoughts during those times. An hour later, a winded Mia Takeda jumped into her car and asked Serena to take her to the nearest bar.

Surprised by the unexpected request, Serena opted to join the woman to keep a close watch on her. Over gin and tonics, she'd learned Mia's story, and they'd become fast friends. Serena had parked her car after dropping Mia off at The Pearl hotel, and quickly jotted down the important points she'd learned. "Ooh, this would make a great novel." She'd tapped the pen on the paper. "Stalker ex-boyfriend thinks Mia wants to marry him. Instead, Mia wants to trap him for all the crimes he's committed. Juicy! Now all I need is a title."

"Serena?" Mia waved her hand. "Are you in there? Maybe I shouldn't interrupt. Did you get an idea for your next book?"

"No." Serena shook her head, coming back to reality. "I was thinking about your wedding day," she lied. "So lovely. Kade is a lucky man," Serena eyed the plate of sweets the server set on the table. "I love this tearoom. Thank you." She grinned at the woman. "May I have a doggie bag in case I don't finish these?"

"Serena," Mia said in a deadpan voice. "You can have all you want. You know that." She looked up at the server. "Send the usual to Ms. Tate's office, Mai. Thanks."

"My pleasure." Mai poured their tea, bowed and left.

The tranquil vibe of the tearoom, the scent of oolong drifting up her nose, finally calmed Serena's nerves. She soaked in her surroundings, studying the setting to make sure she had accounted for every element in the room. The moss green walls were adorned with evenly spaced cherry wood lattice framework, fashioned like windows.

Translucent white paper filled the spaces between the flawlessly polished squares. Matching rectangular lanterns sat in the middle of each guest's table. The design team had chosen seating from the same rich-colored wood, which cast a reddish glow. They had placed lifelike cherry blossom trees against the walls and in strategic corners. Vertical wood beams with intricate gold calligraphy designs were positioned along the walls, making one feel they'd been transported to another world.

The restaurant had three rooms. One for customers who preferred to sit at customary tables and expected typical tea fare, while another had traditional furnishings for high tea. They'd also created a room for private parties. Serena had visited them all. She sat back to admire her favorite round picture frame on the wall. On the white parchment, the artist had drawn a silhouette of a tree with a single pink blossom on one branch. "What did you tell me that was called?"

"A marumado," Mia answered.

"It's my favorite."

"I know." Mia smiled over her teacup.

"Ooh, your grandmother built one heck of a hotel, Mia. I could live here." Serena paused. "Well, I almost do if you count the office Nina so graciously gave me. I'd never have written the book if I didn't get the peace and quiet I needed. The twins are constantly fighting or dancing to loud music."

Mia giggled. "I love them."

"Well, love away, because they'll turn eighteen at the end of next month and go off to college in September."

Serena wiped a tear that had escaped her eye. "Sorry. I didn't mean to get sentimental."

"Children leaving home for the first time is emotional, Serena." Mia poured them another cup of tea. "You're allowed to shed a tear or two."

"Enough about the girls." Serena sat straighter and checked her phone. "They'll be home from school in an hour, so we have time to discuss my dilemma. Plus, I'm not working today."

"After *Marry Me Never's* success, you still haven't given up your rideshare job?" Mia narrowed her eyes.

"No, I like it. I can talk to people, tell them my problems and never see them again," Serena said with a deadpan look on her face. "A-a-and, I can make my own hours. Besides, I quit the boring office job. Two jobs are enough." She grinned, showing all her teeth.

"If I remember correctly, during the drive *I* told *you* my problems," Mia said. "You never said a word."

"I based my book on your problems. It's the reason I kept my mouth shut. Your story beat anything I could tell you." Serena slapped her hand on the table, and Mia grabbed the teacups. "That's it!"

"What? You got an idea?"

"No." Serena dropped her head. She lifted her eyes until they met Mia's. "But I realized what motivates me. My muse is reality. One based on actual events. I can embellish them and turn the real experience into an engrossing novel."

"Good luck with that." Mia giggled. "I'm out of ex-boyfriends who are sociopaths."

"What about your friends?" Serena leaned on the table. "Spill the tea."

Mia gave Serena a scolding look. "I don't talk about my friends. They'd have to share their stories with you."

"Would they?" Serena raised her eyebrows.

"No, everyone is married and boring," Mia cringed. "Including me."

"You? You're never boring. Something's always going on. Aren't you holding your fashion show here instead of New York City?"

Mia's aspiration to become a fashion designer, self-nurtured since high school, had come to fruition. Her journey led to her a collaboration with her friend, Jordan Reese, who she'd first met in design school. Determined to follow their shared passion, they made the bold move to New York City to pursue their dream. Serendipity had also played a role when Jordan met Kade Phillips, now Mia's husband, at an art show. Kade became their financial supporter, backing their designs. They'd found their audience and skyrocketed to success. The JorDan and Mia Collection appealed to everyone. They designed high fashion but made affordable pieces, too.

"Yes, I chose to feature our new line at The Pearl. Grandmother is thrilled," Mia answered. "The show is next week. Hey! I have a great idea. Why don't you tag along and watch the process? It might help clear your mind and open it to ideas for your next best-selling novel."

"Ooh, I'd love to watch the models in action. They're walking on an outdoor runway in the back garden, right?

Hope one of them doesn't end up in that reflecting pool." Serena giggled. "I know I would."

"You wouldn't." Mia shook her head. "Come to the hotel after the girls leave for school tomorrow." Her eyes lit up. "Oh! Grandmother is coming this way, and she seems to be on a mission."

* * * *

Nina Takeda, a formidable woman who commanded attention in any room, was slightly over five feet tall. Her chignon bun always appeared neat, and she never had a hair out of place. With a flair for fashion, Nina always looked as if she'd stepped off a runway. She had her nails done to perfection, never a chip or the wrong color. Serena guessed Nina was in her mid-seventies, although her face barely showed a wrinkle.

"Mrs. Takeda, please join us?" Serena gestured to an empty seat.

"Just for a minute," Nina replied, gracefully sliding into the chair. "And please, Serena, I keep telling you to call me Nina." She placed a napkin on her lap and helped herself to some tea. "I came to give you a message."

"Whoa! The owner of the hotel brought me a message." Serena placed her hand over her heart. "Must be important."

The two women had bonded over their love for Mia. Nina was like her grandmother, too, yet Serena loved to tease her.

"Serena, this is serious." Nina gave her the look only a mother could give a child to get them to behave.

"Okay, what is it?" Serena felt the blood rushing through her veins.

"You have a delivery at the front desk…from Justice."

"What?" Serena waved her hand in the air, pretending the news didn't bother her. "That's it? Your big news?" She hastily gathered her phone and purse. "I've got to go."

"No," Mia said. "Stay and talk."

"The girls…"

"Won't be home for another hour."

"I need time to myself, Mia."

"Where will you go? Don't leave the hotel while you're in this state." Mia pleaded. "Please?"

"I'm going to the pond with those huge goldfish in it," Serena answered. "Okay? But don't follow me."

"They are koi, Serena," Nina said. "And excellent listeners."

"Yes, koi. I knew that. I'm just…" *Flustered.* Serena pushed back her chair and rose from her seat. "Thanks. Good time, Mia. I'll see you tomorrow." She dashed for the exit.

Serena headed down the flagstone path, taking her through The Pearl's lovely Japanese gardens. She only caught glimpses of the lush landscape through her tears. The winding walkway took her to the garden's focal point, the koi pond. According to Nina, it was her favorite spot and an excellent place to think. She plopped onto the bench, and as if they had telepathic knowledge, three koi swam to the surface, staring at her with their intense eyes.

"Nina said she knows each one of you and has given you names," Serena told the fish. "But today, you're mine.

I'm going to name you. Huey, Dewey and Louie. No." She shook her head. "Too easy. Don't worry, I'll come up with something."

Two koi swam away, but a majestic red one with white fins and tail stayed. "Oh, I see how it is. They're loyal to Nina. But you?" Serena pointed to the fish. "Have sympathy for everyone." She threw her head back and blew air through her lips. "Where do I begin?"

When Serena looked at the pond again, the koi hadn't budged. "I loved him, you know. Madly. Passionately." She stared at the fish. "Who am I talking about, you ask? My ex-husband, Justice Tate. He was a bad boy, and I loved bad boys. He owned a motorcycle, and we'd go on day trips, seeing parts of the state I'd never seen before. We had fun together, so much fun. When he asked me to marry him, I think I fainted. Not literally. But in my mind, I did."

The koi's mouth formed in the shape of an "O". He, because Serena decided it must be a male, seemed interested in the story. "You want to hear the rest? It gets uglier. Sadder. I can't really label it."

Other fish swam by, distracting the red and white koi. He turned away but reappeared after a dip underwater. "What do you like to eat?" Serena asked. "Next time I'll come prepared."

The fish seemed to like her statement. Serena swore he nodded. They sat in silence for a moment, and she decided he was waiting to hear more of her sad tale.

"Okay," Serena finally said. "Fine. I'll tell you. We were young when we got married. Twenty-one, to be exact. We had two great years together, then I got pregnant with twins. Girls. Justice wanted to name the girls Jade and Jewel like the shiny, precious gems they were, and so we did. At first, everything was fine. Justice was the typical doting dad. But they cramped his style. We couldn't take off at a moment's notice with a double stroller. That didn't fit on the back of a motorcycle. We needed a practical car. I encouraged Justice to choose whatever he wanted so he'd feel invested. Once the girls started school, I thought things would get better." She paused and shook her head. "Nope." She put emphasis on the 'p'. "They got worse."

Chapter Two

"Jade wanted to play soccer, and Jewel took dance lessons," Serena said to the fish. "After-school activities filled our lives. Justice started to grumble about coming to the games or dropping Jewel off at the studio. To fix things, I told him to use those times for himself, and I'd do the extracurricular stuff. If I planned carefully, I could juggle their schedules. My only request was for Justice to return home in time for dinner." Serena stared straight ahead yet saw nothing. The sound of splashing water distracted her, and she noticed the other two koi had rejoined the red and white one. "Traitors," she muttered. "Go on now. You didn't want any part of this earlier." She waited until they swam away.

"Now where was I?" Serena tapped her chin. "Oh, yes, telling you how my marriage went from bad to worse. Eight years into our marriage, Justice and I began to fight. Something we'd never done. Initially, our arguments revolved around his habitual lateness, but over time, it shifted to Justice staying out all night. When he *was* home, Justice was physically in the home but not present. By the time the girls were ten, I knew our days were numbered."

The red koi dipped underwater and swam in a circle. He returned to the exact spot he'd left and blinked his eyes, as if telling Serena to continue.

"When the twins turned twelve, I called it quits. I was doing everything for the girls and had gotten a full-time job doing what I least liked to do. Filing, typing, answering phones and pretending I had a happy home life. One day I came home to find Justice asleep on the sofa. For some reason, it angered me. He could be loading the dishwasher or folding laundry or cooking a nice dinner. The rage I felt took over, and I rolled him onto the floor, you heard me right, and shook him awake. 'I want a divorce!', I yelled. 'Get out.' And he did. Just like that." Serena snapped her fingers. "No questions. No begging to stay. He left. Boom. It was over."

The fish's shocked expression said it all. It blinked and opened and closed its mouth a few times.

"Did he see the girls, you ask? Only on their birthday and Christmas. He'd text me when he was coming, and that's all the communication we've had. Until now." Serena dropped her head in her hands and cried, trying to stay as quiet as possible.

"It's alright," a woman's voice reassured her, gently resting a hand on Serena's back. "Let it out."

"Nina," Serena whispered.

"I couldn't let you be alone for another minute."

"You watched from afar, didn't you?" Serena gave a humorless laugh. "My life has come down to talking to a fish."

"A very noble one." Nina gestured to the red and white beauty. "I never named him. Nothing ever seemed to fit."

"So, the fish *is* a he," Serena mumbled.

"Yes," Nina answered. "How are you?"

"Confused. Angry. Justice had nothing to do with me until he heard about my book's success. Now he can't wait to connect."

"I don't care about Justice. How do you feel? What do you want?" Nina asked.

"I still love him." Serena made her hands into fists and pounded the top of her legs. "Stupid, huh?"

"Not at all. I was in a similar situation. Kal and I separated for years due to stubbornness and pride."

"Wow, I'm surprised to hear that. You two seem so… solid." Serena shook her head. "Your situation is much different from mine."

"True, but I understand. During all those years of not being together, I still loved Kal. You need to decide if Justice is worth it."

"Worth it?" Serena wrinkled her nose.

"Worth your time and your love, my dear."

"Okay, got it."

"Go to the front desk, Serena. Take the flowers to your office and decide your next step." Nina rose from the bench. "I'm here if you need to talk. So is he." She cocked her head toward the pond and disappeared down a path.

I must look a mess. Serena opened her purse and searched for her compact. She stared at her features in the small mirror. Her brown eyes had flecks of gold, which she highlighted with the perfect eyeshadow. She used the best cream for her face, which kept her honey brown skin smooth and silky. *Not a wrinkle.* Serena liked to change her hair and appearance often, so she kept up with the latest styles. She'd just added a wisp of bangs to her natural, curly look. *Quit stalling. Go to the front desk.*

Serena closed the compact and tucked it in her handbag. She swallowed and stood, straightening her skirt as she did. Proud that she kept her figure after the girls were born, she'd gone up a few sizes over the years. "Size twelve is still good for a forty-one-year-old woman," she said under her breath.

When Serena reached the front desk, the clerk smiled in recognition. "I see Mrs. Takeda found you."

"Yes." Serena placed her hands on the counter. "She said I received flowers."

"We took them to your office," the clerk replied. "It was a huge bouquet, and I don't think you could have seen around it." He chuckled.

"Thanks." Serena nodded and headed down the corridor which led to The Pearl's offices.

Nina had urged Serena to personalize the space and make it a cozy place where she'd feel comfortable writing. A decorator was on standby, ready to help when needed, and all Serena had to do was provide links to her chosen items. She'd typed 'Colors that help boost productivity' into her search engine and debated over warm gray-beige, dark blue, warm white, earthy green or soft pink. Nina's words had come back to her as she studied the colors.

Make it your own. Serena settled on coral and peach with white accents.

As Serena entered the office, a huge spray of flowers greeted her. The staff had placed it on her dark coral desktop, which was long enough for extra objects. "Oh, my." She took a step back. "That must have cost a fortune."

White roses, Serena's favorite, were the focal point of the arrangement. They symbolized young love and innocence, and she naively thought they represented her relationship with Justice all those years ago. "Such a trusting child," Serena sniffed. "Let's see if there is a card."

Serena slid her desk chair over to the bouquet and sat in front of it. A small envelope protruded from the flowers on a green plastic holder. She tugged on the stick until it slipped out and stared at the white paper. "This might not be from Justice. How did he know to send it here? That's it! It's not from him. I have a secret admirer." Serena giggled at the thought.

Once she opened the note, her daydream would end. "One more minute," she told the stick, twirling it in her hand. "Okay. Done." Removing the card from the envelope, she read aloud, "Thinking of you, baby. Congrats on your book's success. Call me. Hope you still have my number. Justice." Tossing the card on the desk, she hissed, "Oh, yeah, *baby*, I've got your number."

* * * *

"Serena, you called!" Justice's husky voice came through loud and clear on her phone.

"My parents taught me to be polite. Thank you for the flowers and how the heck did you know to send them to The Pearl?"

"Wow. Was that a thank you and a scolding rolled into one?"

Serena bit her lip to keep from laughing. "Just tell me."

"I speak to our daughters, Serena. You know that."

"Twice a year."

"No. More than that. They're grown, baby. Jade and Jewel have phones and know how to text. We talk every day."

"Every day?"

"At least once a week."

"Mm-hmm."

"Would you buy once a month?"

"More like it, and they probably text you."

"I can't believe they'll graduate from high school this year, Serena. We did a good job."

We? "Will you come to their graduation? Their eighteenth birthday party?"

"Of course. Why wouldn't I? When is graduation? Is the party on their birthday or another day?"

"You ask a lot of questions, Justice, that you should already know the answers to, especially if you talk to the girls." Serena's heart pounded, and she took a deep, calming breath. "I'll text you with the dates, just like the girls do."

"Hey, before you hang up, how about a drink sometime? We could celebrate you taking the book world by storm."

Serena wrinkled her nose. "Did you look that up? I never heard you talk that way before."

"I even read your book."

"You did?"

"Yes. *Marry Me Never* by Serena Tate."

"Then you know all about sociopathic exes."

"Don't put me in that category." Justice chuckled. "That guy Roman got what he deserved."

"Seems like you *did* read the book," Serena mumbled.

"So, drinks?"

"So, no," Serena answered. "Stop sending flowers and only contact me if it's about the girls."

"Message received." Justice sounded dejected.

Don't feel sorry for him. "Again, thank you for the flowers.' Serena disconnected the call and reached for one white rose. She brought it to her nose and inhaled. "At one time, I would have bought what you're selling, but never again. I love you, Justice, and I wish I didn't." She stuck the flower back into the bouquet. "You didn't send this arrangement to the old me. You wanted to connect with Serena, the author. The one whose face, and book, is all over social media. That's what hurts the most."

* * * *

A knock against her open door startled Serena.

"Serena, may I come in?" Mia's voice floated into the room.

Serena spun her desk chair to face the doorway. "Yes, come through, as they say in the British crime shows I watch."

Mia sat on the pale peach loveseat opposite Serena. "Grandmother thought you could use some company, unless…" She gestured to the computer. "An idea came to you."

"No." Serena slumped in her chair and thrust her thumb over her shoulder. "Those flowers are from Justice. I called and thanked him."

Mia widened her eyes. "You didn't."

"Among other things." Serena shook her index finger at Mia. "I'm perfectly aware of why he sent the flowers. Don't look at me like that."

"I'm not." Mia tried to smile but failed. "The arrangement is beautiful." She paused. "Do you want to talk about Justice?"

"No, I handled the situation." Serena rocked in her chair. "But I still want to discuss something. Set the record straight."

"Oh? Okay."

"Remember the first time we met and went drinking?"

"Vividly."

"You never questioned why a rideshare driver would drink on duty, especially since I'd drive you home. Besides, it was only three in the afternoon."

"I never thought of that," Mia stated. "I was so wrapped up in my problems, I didn't take notice. How many drinks did we have?"

"Two. Mine were virgin."

"Virgin gin and tonics?" Mia cocked her head. "So tonic and lime?" She giggled.

"Yes. Safety first is my motto."

"Well, I thank you for that," Mia said. "But why are you telling me after all this time?"

"I want you to see me as trustworthy. Someone you can count on. Not a person who'd go day drinking, then drive a car."

"I trust you, Serena." Mia stared at the floor. "Oh, I get it. Speaking with Justice brought up trust issues."

"Right. While we're on the subject, anything you need to tell me?" Serena teased.

Mia shifted in her seat and shook her head. "No."

"Okay, don't be so serious. I wanted to lighten the mood, and it seems I brought it down."

"You didn't." Mia assured her. "Besides checking on you, I needed to firm up our schedule for tomorrow. Practice will begin at nine a.m. sharp. Feel free to mingle with the models, interview the staff or whatever might help with your next story. I asked everyone to cooperate."

"You did? This is so kind of you. Hopefully an idea will come to me." Serena lightly clapped her hands. "No one minds me being there?"

"Who, you? The newcomer to the writing world who wrote the hit novel, *Marry Me Never*? Some are dying to meet you."

"Please, I'm blushing."

"You should be proud, Serena." Mia stood to leave.

Serena studied Mia's tiny figure and asked, "What size are you, if I may politely ask? A zero?"

"I wear a two most of the time," Mia said.

"What about the models?"

"Zero or two, but as you know, I have a plus size collection."

"What size are those models?"

"Model. I only have one at this time. I'm growing that portfolio. She's a size sixteen."

Oh, my gosh! Only two sizes up from me. "That's plus size?'

"In the fashion world, yes. Sorry."

"Don't be sorry, Mia, you didn't make the rules. You are trying to break a few, though."

"Thanks. I hope to add more models of that size in the fall."

"When you showcase spring and summer clothes." Serena pursed her lips. "Still wrapping my head around the concept. Fall fashion week is spring wear, and you'll have fall and winter looks at your show for next season."

"You've got it. We're always working ahead." Mia checked her watch. "Jordan should arrive any minute, and I must meet up with him. He's bringing the last of our designs from New York."

"Why isn't he here helping?" Serena asked.

"He is working…in New York."

"Where the boyfriend is." Serena lifted one side of her mouth. "Why doesn't Jordan bring him here?"

"Carlo is too much of a distraction for Jordan. Once here, he wants to focus on work. Carlo will come out the day of the show."

Good, old Jordan. Let Mia do the heavy lifting. "Can't wait to see him," Serena said, giving Mia a salute as her friend left the office.

Chapter Three

Organized chaos surrounded her. Serena avoided workers carrying items to the outdoor runway as she maneuvered her way through the hall. She evaded the photographers positioning their cameras and dodged models hurrying in and out of the reception hall. The staff had set up a dressing room for the models in the bride's accommodations, causing them to rush through the reception hall to reach the stage. In the middle of it all, Mia appeared relaxed and in charge. She spotted Serena and held up her hand in greeting.

"You came!" Mia exclaimed. Distracted for a moment, she directed a confused delivery person to the correct station. "Sorry." She turned to Serena. "I'm trying to keep everything running smoothly. We're setting up a buffet for the afterparty and putting finishing touches outdoors. The decorations need to be in place so we can start rehearsal." She glanced over her shoulder. "I wish Jordan would hurry."

"He's still in his room?" Serena asked. "I could get him."

"No, he promised to come down as soon as he redoes one last design. He wasn't happy with the hemline."

"Working right up to the last minute, I see. That's dedication." Serena refrained from rolling her eyes. Jordan might be Mia's bestie, but she didn't trust the man. She pictured him lying on the bed, scrolling through his phone. He took advantage of Mia, and Serena didn't like it one bit.

"One more thing." Mia touched Serena's forearm. "Lily's here."

"Lily Nichols?"

"Yes, she will oversee the technical side of the show. It's her specialty."

"I know, but doesn't she live in Colorado? Her husband runs a tech company there."

"Correct. But they're both here for the near future. Gabe and Kade are best friends. They grew up together and can't stay apart for too long." Mia giggled.

"I didn't know that," Serena replied.

"Kade and Gabe have some extensive project they're working on, which frees Lily to work with me. Would you watch for her? She should be here any minute. In the meantime, take a tour of the venue." Mia disappeared into a sea of people, and Serena never had time to thank her.

Where should I start? Ooh, that cameraperson looks frazzled. I'll offer my help. Serena headed in the man's direction. "Hi, excuse me, I'm Serena Tate…"

"Yes, yes, Serena Tate." The slim, nervous man, a few inches taller than Serena, stopped fumbling with the camera lens and stuck out his hand. "A pleasure to meet you. I've been meaning to read your book, but with all this going on, I'm overwhelmed."

"I see that." Serena gave him her friendliest smile. "May I ask why you are…?" She twirled her forefinger in the air.

"Upset? Flustered? I'm Ted Lewis, by the way. My friends call me Teddy."

"Well, Ted, nice to meet you."

"You can call me Teddy."

"Fine. Teddy." *Friends already?* Serena bit her lip, a habit she'd had most of her life, to keep from laughing. "Anything I can do to help?"

"Do you know Ava Taylor?" Teddy checked the room with an uneasy gaze as if she'd appear in a puff of smoke.

"From photos, yes. She's a top model." Serena winced, not sure if her answer was correct. Her girls had shown her photos and videos of models, but Serena had no interest and didn't know one model from the other.

"A supermodel," Teddy corrected. "A highly paid fashion model." He leaned closer to Serena. "She thinks she's the boss of everyone." He dropped his voice. "No one likes her."

"A difficult supermodel. Who knew?" Serena nodded. "What can I do? Ask her to be nicer?"

"If you see her coming, let me know," Teddy answered. "She wants to critique every photo I take. I can't do anything right in her opinion. Do you know how many hours I've wasted reshooting her when I already have perfectly good photos?"

I hope that was a rhetorical question. "Does Mia get a say?"

"No. It's in Ava's contract. She gets the first right of refusal no matter who hires me."

From the corner of her eye, Serena noticed a tall, sleek beauty headed their way. She walked as if on a runway. *Obviously, a model.* Her long caramel brown hair had natural golden highlights. Parted to one side, it draped enticingly over one of her shimmering green eyes.

"Teddy, my dear man!" Ava said when she reached them. "I'm surprised Mia hired you for the shoot. I guess she couldn't get Raphael to fly in from New York City." She placed her hands on his shoulders. "I'm sure you'll do fine."

That's insulting. "Hi," Serena said, offering her hand. "I'm Serena…"

"Tate. I heard." Ava sneered. "Sorry, I don't have time to read books."

"And I don't have time for fashion shows," Serena snapped back. "But I'm here."

"Good one." Ava pointed at her. "You're feisty. What are you doing with *him*?"

"Offering my assistance, but Teddy doesn't need it. He's good to go, right?" Serena slapped him on the back a little too hard, making his head bob forward. She noticed beads of sweat forming along his shaved hairline. "Right, Ted?" she asked again.

"Oh, yes. Right." Teddy grabbed his equipment bag with a trembling hand. "If you'd excuse me, I need to set up outside."

Serena faced Ava. "So, do you walk first or last?"

"Both. And a few in between." Ava's eyes darted around the room. "Ooh, I see one of the fashion editors from *Ciao Bella*. I must speak with him."

"Sure, don't let me stop you," Serena mumbled.

"Serena?" A familiar woman's voice caused her to turn. "Lily!"

Although Lily said she highlighted her mousy brown hair to give it some wanted flair, she didn't need to do anything to make herself shine brighter. Her personality won everyone over. She had skillfully pulled her hair into a high ponytail, emphasizing her beautiful, oval-shaped face and perfectly proportioned lips. Wearing a baby blue t-shirt, skinny jeans and black boots, Lily had come dressed for work. Her tortoise-shell glasses slipped down her nose as she hurried toward Serena.

"I *loved* your book," Lily said, throwing her arms around Serena.

Besides being a tech nerd, Lily loved to read. Any genre. Any decade. She even named her dog, Daisy, after the main character in *The Great Gatsby*.

"You *will* sign it?" Lily asked, stepping away from Serena.

"Of course." Serena smirked as she looked around the room. "Is this crazy or just me?"

Lily glanced over her shoulder and looked back at Serena. "It's crazy." They laughed and rolled their eyes. "I need to check the sound system by the runway. Care to join me?"

"I'd love a change of scenery." Serena followed Lily to the opened wall that led to the gardens, taking in the sights and sounds as they walked past tables full of flowers and décor for the event.

One could view The Pearl's back garden through a glass wall, which consisted of multiple panels. The glass could be folded, accordion style, to create an opening of one's choosing, depending on the weather. Today, they were pushed all the way back.

Lily walked into the garden and said, "I got married here." She faced Serena. "So did all my friends," she said under her breath. "But we're not here to talk about me. I heard you're looking for an idea for a new book. Are you a plotter or pantser?"

Serena wrinkled her brow. "Pantser? If I'm guessing correctly."

"You never heard the term?" Lily asked. "Plotters are organized writers. They make outlines and determine what will happen in every chapter before they begin to write. Pantsers just start putting words on a page. Like in the word 'pantser', they fly by the seat of their pants."

"I never heard it put that way. Well." Serena tapped her chin. "Maybe both? For my book, I took an actual situation, which would fall into the plotter category, and added my take as I went along. So, a pantser when I started writing."

A woman, screaming profanities, interrupted their conversation. "Will you please move?" she bellowed.

Serena recognized the voice. "Ava Taylor," she whispered.

"You met her?" Lily widened her eyes.

"Yes. Not too friendly. Let's go rescue whoever she is yelling at."

"Although I'd love to meet her, you go," Lily answered. "I must tend to my duties. Talk later?"

"Absolutely." Serena rushed toward the catwalk, hoping Ava Taylor might be her next story. *Is she a female Roman like the character in my book? A sociopath or a narcissist? Did the sociopath thing. I'll make her a narcissist. She can do all kinds of nasty things in the book.*

A woman, perhaps a size larger than Serena, stood on the runway, hands on hips. "I have every right to practice, Ava. Just like you."

"Excuse me?" Serena waved her hand since she was three feet below them on the path around the reflecting pool.

"What do you want?" Ava narrowed her eyes as she glanced downward. "Oh. You."

"Yes, it's me. Hi." Serena turned to the other woman. "I'm Serena Tate."

"I'm Natalie Grey."

"Nice to meet you, Natalie."

"The *plus*-size model," Ava informed Serena, flaring her nostrils. "She has two changes. I have five. I need the space to figure out my moves."

"And I don't?" Natalie asked.

"Hey, Natalie, mind if we talk for a minute?" Serena asked.

"Okay." Natalie headed down the runway, which sloped to ground level when it reached the reception hall.

The sun cast a golden glow on her auburn hair as she traveled along the ramp.

Serena walked alongside the stage until they met. "Let Ava have her time," she said, connecting with Natalie's baby blue eyes. "Once she's done, I'll make sure you get to walk the entire route." She glanced at the four-foot-wide stage which traveled the total length of the reflecting pool, turned at the end and continued along the other side until it reached the hall.

"How?"

"I know Mia."

"Mia Takeda, the designer, who's putting on the show?"

"Yes."

"Wow, you're lucky. I'd give anything for her to notice me."

"If you're her plus-size model, and I say that lightly, she's noticed you. What size are you?"

"Sixteen."

"Sounds normal to me." Serena did a quick scan of the room. "You stay here, and I'll find Mia."

* * * *

"Well, if it isn't Jor*Dan* in the flesh," Serena said under her breath once she spotted Mia and Jordan studying his tablet.

Jordan insisted on being called Jor Dan, emphasis on Dan, for professional purposes only. He thought the JorDan and Mia collection had a sophisticated ring to it.

Serena couldn't deny he had talent. He did. Yet, in her opinion, Mia did the bulk of marketing and producing their shows. Sure, she had Kade's help, being a movie producer among other things, but Jordan hardly lifted a finger.

"There she is!" Jordan held out his arms to Serena. "I'm in the presence of a famous author. I have goosebumps."

"Stop." Serena gave the man a quick hug.

"Ooh, I heard about the deadly writer's block." Jordan grimaced, then smiled. "It will come. I'm sure of it."

Jordan was a handsome man, clean shaven, oval-shaped face, firm jaw, bright blue eyes. He would change his hair whenever the mood struck him, and when Serena last saw him, Jordan sported white locks for Mia's wedding. The white had made Jordan's blue eyes more noticeable, and he appeared more handsome than ever. He'd chosen light blue for the show, and Serena wondered what color his hair truly was. *I'll have to ask Mia.* He had what her mother would describe as a winning personality and charmed men and women alike. *Except me. He hasn't won my trust.*

"Did I hear a scream?" Mia asked. "Tell me I didn't."

"Don't worry. I took care of it," Serena answered. "Your supermodel wanted her way. Is it possible to distract her so your plus-size model can get on that runway? A-a-and, that girl has no business being called plus-size."

"In the modeling world, she is," Jordan replied. "I'll grab Ava and let you two talk."

"Thanks." Serena waited until Jordan was out of hearing range. "Are you okay? Is he doing any work?"

"Serena," Mia said with a laugh. "We're on track. Jordan oversees the fashion side of the show." She paused. "Now, I want you to meet some models who will walk in the show. I may call upon you to get them in and out of the bride's room without delays." She took Serena's hand and guided her to a group of four tall, slender women of different ethnicities.

"This is Isabella Cruz."

"Nice to meet you." Serena bobbed her head. *Is she the Latina supermodel?*

"Then Ruby Sullivan," Mia gestured to a beautiful Black woman. "Savannah Wells and Aurora Knight." They each had pale skin, appearing to never have met the sun. Aurora was blonde, and Savannah had shiny blue-black hair.

The women surrounded Serena and peppered her with questions about the book. "I could almost fall in love with Roman the way you described him," Aurora said.

"No." Serena shook her head. "You don't want to do that. Sociopath alert."

"I'd take the billionaire any day," Ruby giggled.

"That's the right way to think. Go for the money," Serena teased. She was enjoying the interaction more than the book signings she'd done.

"I think," Isabella said, "The soon-to-be husband sounded a lot like Kade Phillips. Mia's hubby. Was this story based on their life?"

"If you read something into it, it was a mere coincidence," Serena answered, trying not to wince.

"If you say so." Isabella winked.

* * * *

Serena silently observed the room, secretly listening in on conversations and studying people and their mannerisms while she took notes. Music played and stopped, then started up again. People's voices and the beats of different songs mixed, making a pleasant sound. Models flew past her, rushing to the walkway or in the opposite direction. She eventually came upon Natalie sulking at a table by the wall. "Did you get your chance to walk?" she asked, nodding toward the garden.

"For a minute. I barely got to the end of the reflection pool when Isabella got into a fight with Ava." Natalie sniffed. "JorDan has cleared the area for now."

"Wow. I didn't know so much drama happened behind the scenes."

"Oh, there's drama. If Ava had her way, she'd run the show. I wouldn't be here. I'd never get a chance."

"Don't say that." Serena stared out the opening, watching Jordan mediate the fight. *If only I knew what was happening. It could be useful for my book.* "May I ask you something?" She used her kindest voice.

"Yes."

"What are they fighting about?"

"You will not believe this."

"I think I might."

"Who is the star. The number one supermodel. I heard JorDan tell them they both were." Natalie snickered. "Like that would work."

"If you don't mind me asking, who is the most popular?"

"Isabella would like to say it's her, but it's Ava. Ava would have to retire or fall off the face of the earth for Isabella to take the crown."

"Really?" Serena jotted in her notebook. "Interesting."

Chapter Four

"Final rehearsal, everyone!" Jordan spoke into a microphone. "This is the time to work out any kinks, mistakes, blunders and so on."

Mia squeezed Serena's arm. "The week flew by. I can't believe we did it. At first, I thought moving Fashion Week from New York to San Francisco wasn't the best idea, but we have many celebrities attending and are at full capacity. Grandmother is thrilled."

"The girls are, too. They love missing school. Thanks for inviting them to the final rehearsal."

"I wish they could come tomorrow, too, but…"

"Don't apologize. They get to see the fashion. This is more than enough."

"Thanks, Mia," Jade said. "This is wonderful. I'm happy you invited us."

"Everything Jade said." Jewel hugged Mia, and Jade joined in.

Ava strutted into the room, wearing an oversized puffy denim coat which hung past her knees and a rust color chunky sweater dress underneath. Her thigh high boots clicked on the floor as she strutted to the stage. Another model strolled by after a planned interval, and they kept coming dressed in casual attire for fall and winter.

Jade and Jewel clung to Serena's arms, squeezing the life out of them. "Girls, stop," she hissed. "I can't feel my hands. Go sit where I told you and don't move."

Pride filled her as Serena watched her fraternal twins, both five feet nine inches tall, strut like models to their seats as if they'd done it a million times before. One favored Justice, and the other took after her. *They could be models. No! Don't put that in their heads. Education is our top priority.*

"Someone help Stella!" Jordan yelled into the mic. "Dammit, I hope she didn't break an ankle."

Mia turned to Serena. "I've got to check on Stella. Could you let the dressing room know?"

"Sure." Serena rushed from the hall and across the way. Screeching to a halt, she held up her badge to show the security person stationed at the door. Serena made eye contact with the man and her heart slammed against her chest. What was going on behind those seductive brown eyes? Eyes that undressed her in seconds or so she thought they had. She guessed he was over six feet by their close proximity and also noticed the muscled arms below his short-sleeved shirt. *Snap out of it! You have a job to do.* "I need to go in," she said, hoping her voice sounded normal to him. To her, it was an octave higher.

The man nodded and let Serena open the door. "Everyone, may I have your attention?" she yelled, stepping farther into the room.

Men and women in various stages of dress, stopped and stared at her. Dressers held clothes on hangars in the air, mouths agape. Makeup artists and hairdressers put down their tools and turned to her. "I'm sorry to announce this," Serena said, "But Stella, I don't know her last name, turned her ankle and won't walk in the show."

Shocked oohs and aahs came from the group staring at her in horror. *It's not that bad, is it? To a model, I guess. It's their livelihood.* Serena wasn't sure about the turning of the ankle but thought a broken ankle sounded much worse. She'd spared them the bad news until they knew for sure.

Her phone pinged as she turned to leave, and she read the message from Mia. "One more down!"

"Oops, hang on. Another recent development." Serena spun in place to face the still motionless crowd. "One more model won't walk tomorrow. Remember, I'm just the messenger. Mia and Jordan will give you more details."

This time Serena bolted for the door before any more messages of doom could reach her phone. She rushed through the reception hall, heading outside, worried about her girls. The girls were scrolling on their phones when she reached them. "No, you don't," she said in a stern voice. "Do not post what happened here."

"We aren't, Mom." Jewel held up her phone. "Someone already has."

"Darn! Where's Mia?"

"She's coming this way," Jade answered.

Mia pulled Serena aside. "I've got a big ask."

"How big?"

"One where you can say 'no', and I'll understand."

"Ooh, let's hear it."

"Will you allow Jade and Jewel to walk in the show?" Mia cringed and placed her hands together. "They're not eighteen yet, so you must approve. They'll get contracts and pay like the rest of the models."

Serena mulled over the situation. "If they discover they could walk in the show and I said no, they'd never speak to me again."

"They would eventually."

"I guess they would." Serena pressed her lips together. "If I say yes, I'm mom of the year."

"True."

"Which one do I want to be? Bad mom or popular mom?"

"I'm not saying a word," Mia replied, placing her praying hands closer to Serena.

"Fine. But if they mess up, it's on them, not me." Serena grinned.

"Although you're teasing, no one will be blamed," Mia said. "There's no way I can get two models here in time. I need a certain number to show the entire collection." She gestured to the girls who'd been staring at them from their seats. "Do you want to tell them or should I?"

"Girls, come here." Serena waved them over. "Mia would like to ask you something."

"Jade. Jewel." Mia took their hands. "You saw what happened. I need two..."

"Yes!" They squealed, jumping up and down.

"You didn't let her finish," Serena said, closing one eye. "She may want you to sweep up after the show."

"Mom!" Jewel pursed her lips. "Mia would never do that to us."

"But I would." Serena chuckled.

"Mom," Jade said. "We're sorry we didn't let Mia finish." She faced Mia. "Please, go ahead."

"I want you to walk in tomorrow's show. Your mom will escort you to the dressing room for a fitting. I'll get the contracts drawn up and check in with you shortly."

"Contracts? Are we getting paid?" Jewel asked.

"Yes." Mia nodded.

"I'd do it for free." Jade bounced on her toes.

Serena took Mia's hand. "You made their day. Thank you. Before I take them to the dressing room, could I ask you something?"

"What is it?"

"The security man at the dressing room door. Who is he?"

"You mean Jack?"

"I didn't look at his nametag."

"He probably wasn't wearing one." Mia smiled. "Jack Ando works security at The Pearl. He was my grandfather's bodyguard for ten years while he lived in LA. When Grandmother and Grandfather reunited, Granddad moved back here and brought Jack with him."

"He's Asian?"

"Japanese, yes."

"Age?"

"Forty-five?" Mia lifted her shoulder and grimaced.

"Married?"

"For a short time while in his twenties."

"So, kids."

"No." Mia tilted her head. "Hey, wait a minute. Does someone have a crush?"

"I saw him for two seconds, but yes. What else can you tell me?"

"Not much. I am not a matchmaker or know much about those dating sites, Serena. You'd have to check and see if Jack's on one."

"Okay, answer this. Does he have a girlfriend?"

"Not that I'm aware of." Mia shook her head. "But I could find out." She gave Serena a devious smile.

"Oh, my friend, I love you." Serena wrapped her arms around Mia. "This is between us. I don't want the girls to know." She stepped back and looked at Mia. "Are you okay? Losing two models at the last minute is huge. What happened?"

"Oddly, the same thing to both models. The heel broke on one of their shoes, causing them to stumble and twist their ankles."

"Maybe Ava Taylor did it," Serena said, thinking of her book.

"Why would she?" Mia wrinkled her nose.

"To look better than them." Serena saw the twins were impatiently waiting for her. "I better go. Let's discuss this over tea. I'll come back after I take the girls home."

"Okay, I'll break the news to Grandmother. She had a business appointment and couldn't watch the rehearsal. Wait till she hears about the shoes."

"The shoes?" Serena didn't expect that.

"Yes, Grandmother will want to look into it, trust me."

* * * *

When Serena entered the room with Jade and Jewel trailing behind her, it sounded like a catfight had commenced. She heard Isabella, who spoke with her distinctive Spanish accent, raising her voice at another model. "You are jealous of the young ones, Ava. Admit it."

"Why would I lower myself to mess with their shoes?" Ava replied.

"Your reputation is more important than anything," Isabella answered. "Now, two women will not walk in what could be their first show." She put her hand on her hip. "All because of you."

"Or you. How do we know you didn't do it?" Ava shot back. "Your ego is bigger than your head."

"What does that even mean?" Isabella snarled.

"Forget it. Stay out of my sight, Isabella. You like to cause trouble."

A tall, thin man with dark hair and a mustache that curled at the ends stepped between the women. "Please, ladies, let's not get out of control. The show is tomorrow, and we need to work together. Hopefully Mia has found replacements."

"She has," Serena said, moving to a spot where the man could see her. "My girls."

"Your girls?"

"That's correct. My daughters. Whatever Stella and Aurora were supposed to wear, will now be worn by my daughters. Size two."

"Never!" The man threw his hand in the air.

"I know they're not models, but they've practiced walking or strutting or whatever you call it since they were five years old. They wear a size two," Serena repeated for the second time. "Ms. Takeda will be here soon and confirm."

"We shall see."

Mia arrived just in time, holding papers in her hand. "Is there a problem, Enrique?"

"No, Ms. Takeda. Are you sure you want to use untested models?"

"Yes. Now get them dressed so they can practice."

"Come this way, girls." Enrique motioned to a paneled screen, and the trio disappeared behind it.

Serena gave Mia a look of thanks, then rolled her eyes. "Backstage drama."

"It's always like this the closer we get to a show. No big deal." Mia gestured to a table. "Let's sit there. If you have any questions, please ask."

Serena sat to sign the papers and when she got to the salary, she gasped. "Thirty dollars an hour? That's all?" She knew it sounded ungrateful and looked at Mia. "Sorry."

"That's what first-year runway models make, Serena. Being one is not easy. They make anywhere between three to eight hundred dollars per show."

"Except those super ones."

"Sadly, it's the same in any creative profession. The one percent make all the money. Take books, for example. You were lucky. Most authors struggle to get noticed and barely make ten thousand dollars a year and sometimes less."

"You're right. Same for the music industry, actors and other creative industries. We only know a handful of them. It's a tough business."

"Mom?" Jade called. "How do I look?"

Tears welled in Serena's eyes as she inspected her daughter's outfit. Jade wore a short, oversized pale gray sweater dress with a huge turtleneck collar. White boots that ended below her knees and hanging diamond earrings finished the look. Her dark curls, parted down the middle, hung neatly over the sweater's collar.

"Here," Enrique said, giving her a large burgundy handbag. "You'll carry this, too."

Jade, who'd gotten Justice's handsome looks and rich brown skin tone, had transformed into a model before Serena's eyes. She waved a hand in front of her face to keep from crying. "You are a queen, Jade. A queen."

"What about me, Mom?" Jewel stepped from behind the screen wearing a cream-colored buttoned sweater with silver accents over a long glittering silver skirt. Her hair was pulled back into a ponytail.

"My babies," Serena cried. "So beautiful."

"Jordan and I cleared the area," Mia said. "You two have the stage to yourselves. Practice as much as you want. Are you ready?"

"We are so ready," Jewel answered. "Thanks for the opportunity."

* * * *

Nina played with her empty teacup, jiggling it from one edge of the saucer to the other. "Two pairs of shoes malfunctioned?" she asked again. "Did Jack bag them as evidence?"

"Should you even ask that question?" Mia answered. "He did."

"I want to see them."

Mia gave Serena an "I told you so" look. "He took them to the security office. The team will examine them thoroughly and pass them along to the police."

"Your hotel security has the ability to do that?" Serena asked.

"Yes, and much more." Nina nodded.

"Not a regular security force, I take it?" Serena pursed her lips.

"Many of our people have served in the armed forces and developed a variety of skills," Nina answered. "Some were in Special Opps and have unique talents. They do an excellent job. In fact, Jack Ando once worked full-time for the LA police force. When he left the force to guard Kal, I think he missed the job. We encouraged him to apply to the

San Francisco department for part-time detective work, and with his background, they hired him on the spot."

"Wow. Jack's busy." Serena sipped her tea. "No time for romance."

"Serena Tate." Nina widened her eyes. "Are you interested in Jack?"

"Maybe. Does he have a girlfriend? Mia didn't know."

"No, he does not."

"Grandmother," Mia said, placing her hand over the woman's hand. "Makes it her business to know everything about her employees and family."

"Mia!" Nina exclaimed. "You make me sound like a busy body."

"Never, Grandmother." Mia chuckled.

"I thought I'd find you here," a woman's voice said. "May I join you for a minute?"

"Join us for more than that, Lily," Mia said. "How is the technical side of my show going? Hopefully better than the main event."

"Great. No problems. I came to ask about the broken shoes."

"See," Nina said. "Lily suspects something, too."

"Since I'm positioned close to the stage, I thought the heel of Stella's one shoe appeared loose. She'd gone by so fast, I told myself I was seeing things. Then wham, she's on the floor." Lily looked at each one of them. "I watched more carefully from then on. When Aurora hit the stage, I swear I saw the same shoe problem." She accepted a cup of tea from Nina. "Coincidence? I think not."

Chapter Five

Serena could hardly contain her excitement. Not only did she have front row seats, but her girls would walk in the show. Although she would love to be in the dressing room, Serena kept out of the way and paced in a corner of the reception hall. The twins called it hovering when she tried to stay. Reluctantly, she left. Her mind struggled to focus on a book theme, yet she anxiously awaited the start of the show.

"Hello, there," Teddy said, placing his camera bag on the table next to her.

"Hi, Teddy. Good to go?"

"Always. Although." Teddy placed his hand to the side of his mouth. "I hope the show is."

Serena studied the man. She hoped he hadn't sabotaged the rehearsal or anything else. *Why would he? He has nothing against Mia. She hired him. Believes in him.*

"Serena?" Teddy touched her arm. "Are you in there?"

"Oh." Serena shook the thought from her head. "Yes."

"What do you think about what I said?"

"Think?"

"I'll take extra pictures of your girls and give them to you no charge."

"That is very sweet, Teddy, but I'd be happy to pay." *Especially after I saw what working models make. Your salary can't be much better.*

"We can discuss later. Got to set up. See you outside?"

"I wouldn't miss it." After Teddy gathered his gear and headed for the gardens, Serena placed her hands against the wall and took a deep breath.

"You okay, babe?"

"Justice!" Serena dropped her hands and spun to face him. "What are you doing here?"

"The girls invited me."

"They can't invite anyone. Full house. No room."

"Jade texted your friend, Mia, and she gave her approval. I have to watch the show from this room, but I don't care."

"Fine, just stay out of the way."

"I will." Justice took a breath and exhaled. "You've moved up in the world, Serena. Mia Takeda is your friend?"

Serena didn't want Justice to know they were friends, let alone how close they'd become. "We're more like acquaintances."

"Not what I heard. Girls can't stop gushing about the woman."

"They're exaggerating." Serena checked the hall for Mia. *Good. She's not here.*

"How did you meet?" Justice asked.

"I was her rideshare driver. Once my book hit the shelves, she remembered me. Mia invited me to tea to celebrate."

Justice wrinkled his brow. "That is not the story I heard. You have an office here."

"Okay, fine. During the ride, I told her I wanted to write a book and needed a quiet space. Mia proposed I work at the hotel. I pay rent," she lied.

"Was that so hard?" Justice took a step closer, and Serena could smell his cologne. The scent had driven her mad in the past and she'd throw caution to the wind. "Kiss for luck?" He smiled, showing his beautiful straight white teeth.

Serena gave him a quick peck on the lips. *Why did I do that? The cologne made me do it. I'm blaming the cologne.*

Lily's voice came over the speakers, and she asked for people to find their seats. The show was about to start. Hip hop music replaced the voice, and the beat spread through the room.

Serena gave Justice one last look. "They're going to do great, right?"

"How could they not?" Justice threw out his hands. "They're our girls."

"Remember, stay out of the way," Serena said as she left the hall. She walked past Lily sitting behind the soundboard and patted her on the shoulder.

Lily looked up and said, "They'll be fine." As if she felt Serena's nerves.

Her seat was front and center, like Mia had promised, halfway down the stage. Dying to search for celebrities,

Serena forced herself to stare straight ahead. The music changed, signaling the start of the show. Ava Taylor confidently strode by her. She focused on the runway and nothing else. Ava wore the same oversized puffy jeans coat from rehearsal, elegantly showcasing the dress by sliding her hand along the opening. *She's good.*

One by one, the models came in perfect timing until Serena spotted a pale gray sweater dress rising from the ramp. She blinked, and the model came into focus. A beautiful Black woman sashayed down the catwalk. *That's my baby girl.* Serena's heart swelled to the point of bursting. *Stay calm. Don't embarrass her.* She sat on her hands to keep from waving.

As she passed by, Serena swore she saw Jade's pinkie bend in a greeting just for her. She searched her purse for a tissue, refusing to cry in front of this audience. *Oh, what the heck.* Serena dabbed her eyes, then blew her nose.

More models paraded by, and finally Serena spotted Jewel in her shimmering silver skirt and short cream sweater appear at the low end of the stage. She seemed in her element, prancing like a racehorse toward her mother. She, too, gave the finger wave, and Serena realized the girls had planned it. "That's my baby!" Serena exclaimed, rising from her seat.

The audience stayed silent, and Serena timidly returned to her seat. Mia would most likely give her a lecture later, but at that moment, it felt good. Serena glanced to her right and left, expecting the fashion police to eject her from her seat. *Maybe Mia was too busy to notice.*

Round two began, and this time the models wore fall fashion, not chunky sweaters, heavy coats and boots for winter. A theme of ivory, rust and brown dominated the stage, and even in late February, Mia had to be one step ahead. She'd premiered her spring fashion line in September and was likely working on another for next February. *How does she keep up?*

Ava Taylor swept past her in a brown suede jacket, tight rust leather skirt which hung past her knees and ankle boots with three-inch spikey heels. Her third appearance at the event. Serena hardly paid her notice, but turned Ava's way when she heard the crowd gasp. Her ankles wobbled to one side, then the other. A spike heel came off her shoe, causing her balance to fail. Ava's head fell back, and she dropped to the walkway, then her body rolled into the reflecting pool. Water splashed in every direction. With all the clothes she wore, she plummeted to the bottom.

With lightning speed and dexterity, Jordan Reese hopped over the stage and into the shallow water which splashed against his thighs. "Someone, call an ambulance," he yelled, wading through the water to reach the unconscious model.

Jorden swept Ava into his arms as The Pearl's security team arrived on the scene. Two men helped him from the water while Jordan tightly held Ava.

"Stay back," Jordan roared to people congregating around the walkway. He carefully placed Ava on the white floor and began CPR. A security person, who Serena recognized as Doc, began mouth-to-mouth resuscitation.

Once Serena gathered her wits, she searched the walkway for Jade and Jewel. To improve her view, she rested against the stage, but a man's voice and a hand on her shoulder instructed her to move away.

Serena turned, ready to admonish him. Instead, she inhaled his cologne, a lemony sage scent, and looked into beautiful dark brown eyes. She whispered, "My daughters."

"We've taken all the models to the dressing room, ma'am."

Ma'am? "Do not call me ma'am," Serena answered. A fire lit in her belly and her inner mama bear came out. "I need to get my daughters to safety."

"Sorry." Jack Ando held up his hands in surrender. "We need to question the models before we release them."

Serena put one hand on her hip. "So, they're prisoners?"

"Not at all. Just doing my job."

"Ma'am?" Serena closed one eye as she teased him.

"Not saying that again." The corner of Jack's mouth twitched.

"Mia told me you work for the SFPD. You'll work the case?"

"I take care of Pearl business, yes."

"Good. Then, as a favor to me, please take me to my daughters."

* * * *

"Jade! Jewel!" Serena rushed to where they huddled together in the bridal room.

"Is Ava okay?" Jewel asked, a fearful expression on her face.

"I don't know for sure," Serena answered truthfully. "I heard an ambulance. The medics are attending to her now."

"I hope she makes it," Jade said. "We didn't see it happen. Was it awful?"

"Ava appeared to lose her balance like the models did yesterday. Only she didn't stumble like the others. She dropped to the ground. To make matters worse, her body rolled to the edge of the stage and plunged into the pool."

Serena kept watch on Jack Ando, interviewing the models. It looked like he separated them into two groups. *What's that about?* He glanced in her direction, and she quickly turned to the girls. "That nice man is going to talk to you. Be cooperative."

"We're not five, Mom," Jade said. "That nice man?"

"His name is Jack Ando. He's part of the security team at The Pearl. He also works part time for the police department."

"Hmm." Jewel tapped her chin. "Seems like you know a lot about him, Mom. Interested?"

"No. Shh." Serena peeked over her shoulder. "Mia told me about him. And speaking of Mia, you girls called her last night without telling me."

"We knew you wouldn't let Dad come," Jade said. "We wanted to check with Mia before we said anything to Dad or you."

"After you got permission, you said nothing to me." Serena lifted her brows.

"The officer is coming this way," Jewel whispered. "Hello, Mr. Ando. It's nice to meet you."

"How did you…" Jack looked at Serena. "Never mind."

Serena swore he winked, but after taking a second look, he appeared stoic. "Can we help you, officer?" she asked.

"Jack is fine. Since your girls are underage, I'd like you to come with them while I ask some questions."

"Certainly, Jack." Serena plastered a smile on her face and tried to walk the way the models did but failed miserably.

Once seated, Jack said, "Please state your names."

"Jade Tate."

"Jewel Tate."

"Serena Tate."

"Not you." Jack shook his head at Serena.

"Sorry."

"Mia hired you yesterday?" Jack asked, looking at the girls.

"Yes," they answered.

"Did you see anyone who seemed out of place in the dressing room?"

"Besides my mom?" Jade giggled. "Sorry. This is serious. Someone got hurt."

"No, we didn't," Jewel said, nudging her sister.

"Where were you when Ava fell on the stage?"

"In here, changing," Jewel answered.

A knock came at the door, and without pausing for a reply, it burst open. "Detective Ando?" A pale, middle-aged man with a rounded stomach and balding head stepped through the entryway. "May I have a word?"

"Excuse me," Jack said, and joined the man.

"Who's that?" Jade said under her breath.

"Someone from the station?" Serena tried to lipread. "They may have sent someone over when the call came in for an ambulance." She struggled to figure out what they said but only caught one word. *Dead? No, I didn't read that right.* Jack hung his head and shook it from side to side. *Nope, I did.* "Girls, remain calm. Bad news is coming."

Jack hadn't noticed all eyes were on the men during their conversation. He turned to make an announcement, and by his expression, he seemed surprised. "I'm sorry, everyone. Ava Taylor died on the way to the hospital."

A collective gasp went through the room. Sobs and crying followed.

"We must wait for a lab report and the police need to complete their investigation." Jack wiped his face with his hand. "It's a very sad day for all of us."

The short, heavy-set officer stepped in front of Jack. "I'm Detective Bill Mitchell with the SFPD. To clarify, Mr. Ando is saying there's been a murder. No one leaves the premises without our permission. Got it?"

Louder sobs and cries filled the air, and Serena embraced the twins. Their eyes had welled with tears, and they placed their heads on each of her shoulders. "It's going to be alright," she said. "Mia should be here soon."

Jack and the officer continued their private conversation, and Serena discreetly moved closer to listen. She prayed Jack hadn't noticed.

"I've got it covered, Bill," Jack said. "You can return to the station."

"Yeah, I know The Pearl is your jurisdiction, but you're a part-time officer, Jack. You need a seasoned veteran like me to guide you along."

"I'll be fine. I know what I'm doing. Besides, you're not my boss. We're on the same level. Detectives."

"I'm full-time. Been at it almost twenty-five years."

"Let's not play 'List your Credentials' right now. If I need help, I'll call you."

"How about if I check in now and then?"

"Who are you trying to impress?" Jack asked. "The police commissioner? He and Mrs. Takeda are good friends. Do you want her to put a word in for you? I can arrange it."

"How dare you?" Bill's face changed to a shade of purple Serena had never seen. "I'm doing my job. Do yours." He turned on his heels and exited the room.

"Ooh, so Mr. Bill wants a promotion?" Serena asked as Jack walked by.

"What?" Jack narrowed his eyes. "Were you…? Come with me."

The pair returned to where her daughters stood, holding hands and trembling. Serena gave Jack her best pleading look. "Look at them. Two scared kittens. Can they leave? They know nothing."

"You can all leave," Jack answered.

"Oh no, she doesn't!" Isabella Cruz yelled, pointing at Serena. "If I stay, she stays."

"Could you give me a reason?" Jack asked.

"Think." Isabella touched the side of her head. "Yesterday, two models twisted their ankles and couldn't walk in the show. Suddenly, her two daughters take their place. Serena had motive and access to this room. Check the security camera. She probably snuck in here and loosened the heels on their shoes. Ava's, too. She drowned because of you." She jabbed her finger in the air. "You are guilty."

"Whoa." Jack pointed to a chair across the room. "Please, take your seat." He faced Serena. "She has a point."

Serena tried to swallow but it stuck in her throat. She blinked and turned to her girls, gesturing to her mouth. Jade handed her a water bottle. She sipped the cool liquid and turned back to Jack. He looked at her like a suspect, not a future girlfriend. What else could go wrong?

Chapter Six

Serena rapid-fired instructions at the twins. "Girls, I'm sure your dad is still here. I'll have him take you home. Call Grandma and ask her to come and stay the night. Don't tell her I'm a suspect in a murder investigation. Just say I'm working on something and will sleep in my office. Can you do that?"

The twins nodded.

"Let's make sure you heard me." Serena studied their grief-stricken faces to see if they listened. She longed to embrace them and assured them everything was fine, even though it wasn't. "Do not tell Grandma a thing. You'll give her a heart attack."

"We won't, Mom." Jewel threw her arms around Serena's neck and whispered in her mother's ear. "Isabella is a bitch. She's trying to put the blame on you, so she doesn't look guilty. She was always fighting with Ava in here."

"Thanks for the info," Serena whispered back. She made eye contact with Jack and asked, "May I go look for my *ex*-husband?"

"You may but bring him here so I can question him before they leave."

"Of course."

Once out the door, Serena pushed the girls in Justice's direction. "Go explain everything to your dad. I must find Mia."

As she walked around the venue, it felt like an out-of-body experience. Serena didn't belong there. She should be safely tucked away in her office, writing her new book. But, no. Amidst all the glamour and glitz, she'd become a suspect in a murder case. She walked right into Lily without seeing her. "Oh, I am so sorry," Serena said. "Lily!" She hugged the woman. "I need your help."

Lily never flinched as Serena relived her story. "Why are you not surprised?" Serena asked.

"I've heard worse." Lily smiled and patted Serena's upper arm. "I'll get access to the security footage and review it."

"There's one thing I left out," Serena said. "I snuck into the dressing room before the last rehearsal. Curiosity got the best of me. I wanted to see the fashion."

"Was anyone else there?" Lily asked, widening her eyes.

Serena hung her head. "No."

"That makes you appear more guilty."

"Guilty of what?" Mia asked, approaching the pair.

"Murder," they answered.

"No, no, no. A thousand times, no." Mia shook her head after Lily and Serena relayed what had happened.

"This is ridiculous. Isabella accused you of sabotaging the shoes so your girls could walk in the show?"

"I'm afraid so," Serena answered. "Will you join me in the dressing room and speak with Jack?"

"I'll come as quickly as I can."

"One more favor." Serena glanced in the twins' direction.

"Anything."

"The girls went to find their dad. They'll bring him over to you and probably ask where I went. Stall for time while I go to my office and get my journal. Since I'll be here for some time, I can write down my ideas."

"Ooh, you're going to start your next book," Lily said with a light clap of the hands.

"Not really. I want to enter some thoughts while they're fresh in my mind."

"Hey, wait a minute," Mia said. "All of this," she waved her hand around in a circle, "Should have given you an idea for your book. You told me you needed something real to happen for you to be inspired. Isn't this the perfect scenario?"

"You mean *The Model's Murder*?" Serena asked, lifting a brow.

"Terrible title," Mia answered.

"Agree." Lily avoided her gaze.

"It's a working title," Serena said. She noticed Justice and the girls heading their way. "Mia. Lily. That's my ex, Justice, with the twins. I can't stay for introductions but keep them busy until I return."

* * * *

Serena checked right and left before dashing down the hall to her office. "Please don't see me, Jack Ando," she whispered. Saying his name set off a flight of butterflies in her stomach. "Made it." Unlocking the door, she relocated the sofa to the far corner of the office. "There. This is a perfect wall for my detective board."

Her computer beckoned. She entered names of models who might have motive to eliminate Ava or at least get her out of the way. Isabella Cruz came to mind. She printed off pictures of her and Ava to place on the wall. *Think!* Who else had she met? *Ruby. Natalie, Savannah, Aurora.* "What the heck. They might be guilty." She easily found photos of the models.

Serena drummed her fingers on the desk. "The photographer. Teddy." *Ted Lewis.* She typed the name. No photographers with his name. "Hmm, what name do you go by, my friend?" She tried Teddy Lewis but still no hits. "Ted is short for Theodore. I'll try that."

This time, Serena hit pay dirt. She studied Theodore Lewis' profile. Late thirties. Single. Had some difficulties in his professional career due to drug use. "Bingo! Did Teddy drug Ava?"

Serena hit print as her phone pinged. "It's Mia." She read the message. *Where are you?*

One more minute. Serena typed back. She stared at the computer, willing her fingers to do what they must. Reluctantly, she printed a picture of Serena Tate. The one she liked from the back of her book. She gathered the photos from the printer and put them on the counter. "I need a corkboard and push pins. Some yarn. Different colors."

Serena created her wish list and sent it off to the purchasing agent who always ordered supplies for her office. She asked if someone could get the board installed on the designated wall ASAP. Grabbing her notebook and pen, she took off at a quick pace toward the hall.

"I'm back." She announced, taking shortened breaths as the group stared at her. "Sorry I wasn't here for the introductions."

"Mom, where have you been?" Jade asked.

"Just getting something from my office. This way, please." Serena motioned for her family to follow her. She wanted to get Justice away from Mia in case he started asking personal questions.

"It's about time," Jack said when they entered the room.

From the look of the place, Serena noticed he'd interviewed more models. A greater number of people filled one side compared to the other. *Who stays, and who goes?*

Jack pulled Justice away from the group, and Serena inched closer.

"Serena," Jack said sternly. "Please wait with your girls."

"Fine. I wanted to make sure you knew Justice is my *ex*-husband."

"Ex. Got it." Jack nodded, and Serena noticed his twitch of a smile again.

"Girls, get away from here," Serena said. "Detective Ando has a job to do."

"Mom," Jewel said with an exasperated sigh. "*You* need to join *us*. Not the other way around."

"I hope he lets you go home," Serena said when she joined the twins. "You did nothing wrong."

"Neither did you," Jade answered. Her shoulders slumped. "I never dreamed our first modeling gig would end like this."

"First and last," Serena said, closing one eye and pointing at her. "College, here you come."

"What if we went to college in New York?" Jade asked in an eager voice. "We'd be close to Mia, and she could use us whenever she needed us."

"Mia plans to live at The Pearl for the near future. She won't be in New York. Besides, Santa Clara has already accepted you. Far enough away, but close if you need me."

"It's an hour away," Jewel moaned. "We agreed to it because you let us stay on campus, and we got partial scholarships."

"Brains over beauty, girls," Serena said. She checked on Jack and Justice and saw they were still talking.

To help ease the tension, Serena pretended they were fighting over her. Justice rubbed his goatee as he discussed something serious. His hand skimmed over his braided hair to make a point. Jack's clean-shaven look and military-style haircut, long on top, short on the sides, suited him. He held his ground, peppering Justice with questions. Justice was an inch taller, but Serena bet Jack would win in a fight. Not that she wished for a brawl.

"Mom." Jewel nudged her. "Does it look like they're done?"

Serena nodded. "They must be finished. Dad is coming this way."

"I can take the girls home, Serena, but you must remain here. Sorry." Justice took her by the shoulders and brought her to his solid chest for a hug. "I'll stay with them."

"No need. My mom is coming."

"I'll wait until she arrives." Justice kissed her cheek when he let her go. "You don't need to worry. I'm here for you and the girls."

"Really?" *No, don't fall for his 'I'll do anything for you' routine.* Serena shot a 'Did you call, grandma?' look at the girls.

Jewel instantly turned away, phone to her ear. After finishing the call, she faced Serena and said, "Grandma can arrive in two hours."

"I'll feed them and put them to bed," Justice said.

"We're not babies, Dad," Jade said, rolling her eyes.

"He's missed a lot of years, girls," Serena replied. "Things change, Justice."

"How about if we stop at your favorite fast-food place and buy whatever you want?" Justice smirked at Serena.

"Just get them home safely," Serena said, hugging the girls. "I love you both, more than you know. I'll keep in touch."

"How long do you think this will take?" Jewel asked.

"I have no idea, baby girl. Lily and Mia are here. They won't let anything happen to me."

"What about Mrs. Takeda?" Jewel asked. "She'll have your back."

"I'm not sure if Nina knows yet," Serena answered.

"I think she does." Jewel gestured toward the entryway. "There she is."

* * * *

"Jack, may I have a word?" Nina asked.

Serena escorted her family to the door and returned to the spot where she'd stood for the last hour. Jack had never told her where to sit. *Where will I be? Left side of the room or the right?* She hoped this would end soon, and they'd move on to the next step of the interrogation.

The conversation finished, and Nina approached Serena. "Tea room, table in the far corner," she whispered so softly that Serena almost missed the directions.

"I can leave?"

"As long as you stay in the hotel," Nina answered.

"Before I go to the meeting, I need to find Lily."

"She'll be there."

"You know what happened?" Serena chuckled. "Of course, you do."

"Go."

Serena checked to see if Jack watched her movements, but he was interviewing another model. She exited and headed for the back entrance to the gardens. Last summer, over tea, Nina had told her the history of The Pearl hotel and its gardens.

Nina and her brother Kaito had nurtured a dream of building a hotel since childhood. Three decades ago, their youthful aspirations transformed into a remarkable reality. Amidst the bustling construction phase, Kaito had brought a sketchpad and colored pencils to the site. With his eye for design, he drew as he spoke about the possibilities for the gardens, producing wonderful pictures from his words. His creative side always amazed his sister, while her organizational and analytic skills awed him. They worked well together and dreamed of crafting a space which would captivate any visitor, hoping guests would return when in the city. Their dreams came to fruition. The gardens earned a spot on the coveted top ten attractions in San Francisco.

Since she entered the back way, Serena walked on the path which led past a shrine. Kaito insisted the front entrance have a red Torii gate, then Nina reminded him it must lead to a shrine. Decorative before he died, it now held Kaito's ashes. "Hey, Kaito." Serena waved as she passed by. She continued to the garden's center and stopped at the koi pond. As if he knew, the red fish with the translucent white fins and tail surfaced from the water.

Serena leaned towards him and said, "I'm working on a name for you, but I need to get to a meeting." She jutted her thumb over her shoulder. "Tearoom." He appeared to understand. "We'll talk later." She gave the fish a thumbs up and continued down the path.

Lily waited at the entrance and lifted her hand in greeting when she spotted Serena. "I've got the footage," she whispered, linking arms with Serena. "Mia is at the table."

A server brought afternoon tea and a tier of small sandwiches and tiny desserts. "We made a special blend today," she said, pouring each woman a cup. "Darjeeling First Flush tea. I hope you like it."

Lily waited until the server departed, then arranged her phone to display the footage. "Serena, you said you entered the room prior to the last rehearsal," she said. "I started there." She pressed play, and the empty hallway in front of the dressing room came into view.

A woman snuck onto screen looking over her shoulder, one way, then the other. She tiptoed up to the entrance and opened the door.

"Is that me?" Serena screeched. "It can't be. I don't tiptoe."

"Shh, keep it down," Mia scolded.

"*Oh*, it's *you*, Serena," Lily snorted. "And you're definitely tiptoeing." Her expression shifted to a more serious demeanor. "This doesn't look good."

"Start the dressing room footage," Serena demanded.

"The hotel doesn't film inside rooms," Lily answered. "Not fair to the bride or people changing clothes."

"Will Jack see this?" Serena asked.

"Eventually." Mia winced.

"How do I defend myself? I didn't touch any shoes." Realization hit her. "Wouldn't my fingerprints be on the shoes?"

"Yes," Mia replied. "I'm texting Jack now. I'll ask if our team can thoroughly examine the shoes before sending them to the police department."

"Girls," Serena locked eyes with Lily, then Mia. "Thank you. I love you both. I've got a big ask, and it's okay to say no." She inhaled deeply, then let it out. "Will you help me solve this crime and clear my name?"

"Already there," Lily said.

"On board." Mia nodded.

"All we need is a name for our team," Serena said. "And I already have one."

Mia and Lily groaned.

"Please don't say Charlie's Angels or something similar," Lily said.

"How about Partners in Crime? P.I.C. When we exchange messages containing those three letters, it means we need to meet in this wonderful tearoom."

"If possible." Mia added.

"Okay, if possible," Serena said. "You in? Partners in Crime?"

Lily looked at Mia. "It is a good way to stay in touch. No one else will know what the code means."

"Makes sense," Mia answered. "We're in this together. Partners in Crime. Let's clear Serena's name."

Chapter Seven

"The queen has arrived," Serena whispered.

Nina Takeda did not hurry. She had a regal walk and used it to her advantage. Stopping at the check-in podium, she chatted with the host. While moving through the room, Nina acknowledged servers with their hands full of trays or carrying teapots. Others, who didn't, got a pat on the shoulder or a quick chat.

When Nina arrived at the table, she gracefully slid into the empty seat. Without mincing words, she said, "I was with Jack when your text arrived, Mia. He's sorry to say all the evidence has left the building. He called the department and requested that the lab tests the shoes first." She turned to Serena. "Jack has let some models and staff return to their rooms. The rest are to report to the bar off the main restaurant. That includes you, Serena."

"The bar?" Lily chuckled. "Are drinks allowed?"

"Non-alcoholic ones. The kitchen can easily bring in food, and we can seal off the area," Nina answered.

"Makes sense." Lily paused. "Anything I can do to help? I'd love to go to the bar and check out the suspects."

"Not everyone is a suspect, Lily," Nina answered. "Some are witnesses with pertinent information. I don't think Jack will let you in the bar during his questioning, but I have something I'd like you to investigate."

"Anything."

"Get additional security footage and extend the timeframe. Try to identify any person who entered at odd hours. This might take you a while."

"On it." Lily scooted back her chair. "Good luck, Serena. Stay in touch if possible."

"Thanks, Lily." Serena looked at the remaining women. "I better get to the interrogation room."

"Serena." Mia smirked. "It's not that bad. We'll get your name cleared soon."

"Good, because once it is, I'll help with this investigation until I find the killer, whether or not Jack likes it."

* * * *

Nina offered to walk with Serena to the bar. They stopped at the pond, and the red koi sprang from the water.

"He is happy to see you, Serena," Niina said. "Have you thought of a name for him?"

"Actually, I have." Serena smiled. "I hope he likes it."

"I'm sure he will." Nina patted Serena's back. "Go on, child, tell us. We are on pins and needles."

Serena teared up at her words. In Nina's eyes, family and friends of the next generation were her children, and she was glad to be among them. "Samurai," she said. "Sam for short."

"Ahh." Nina nodded. "A noble name. They were legendary Japanese warriors and gave their undying loyalty to their feudal lords." She pointed to the fish, swimming circles in the water. "I believe Samurai likes his name."

"Do you, Sam?" Serena blinked back more tears. "One question before we go, Nina. What do koi eat? I promised Samurai I'd bring him something good to eat."

"A wonderful question, Serena."

"Also, are guests allowed to feed them?"

Nina gestured to a sign by the pond. It asked people not to throw food or coins in the water, and if they wish to feed the koi, the Good Luck store sold the appropriate food.

"Oh." Serena read the sign again. "They eat special food." She had visited the lovely shop that sold good luck charms and souvenirs and would stop in once the investigation ended.

"Not really." Nina chuckled. "The sign is there for the koi's protection. They eat just about anything. If these koi lived in a natural habitat, they'd eat tiny insects, plants and algae at the bottom of a pond. We sell koi food to keep the fish safe. Between you and me, the koi love honey nut oats."

Serena wrinkled her brow. "Like the oat cereal in the box?"

"They prefer the honey nut kind."

"Hey, Sam," Serena called. "It's my favorite, too." She turned to Nina. "What else can they eat?"

"People food. They love cereal, lettuce, shrimp, rice and peas. Anything we like, they like. The Sushi House feeds them leftovers from the day. But we must not feed them food high in carbs. They have a hard time digesting them."

"Like the models." Serena bit her lip.

"Serena." Nina gave her a hug. "I will take my leave. Jack is expecting you shortly."

If only for the right reason. "Thank you, Nina," Serena answered, and followed the path which led her out of the gardens.

* * * *

"Well, look who decided to join us," Jack said, sweeping his hand toward a line of people. "With your consent, we'd like a copy of your fingerprints." He stepped closer and said under his breath. "I should have the shoe results in no time." Jack returned to where he'd stood so quickly, Serena thought she'd dreamed it.

I didn't make that up. He said it. He cares. Jack likes me. He really likes me. "Thanks for the info." Serena gave her best sunny smile as she got behind the last person in line. "Will this exonerate me, Jack?"

"I'm afraid not," he answered. "But it's a step closer to eliminating you as a suspect."

Curious to see who oversaw the fingerprinting, Serena struggled to look around the line of people. Standing behind a table, Detective Bill Mitchell appeared to be in his element. His gruff voice gave succinct orders, and he kept the line moving.

Since she was last in line, Jack stood near her. "He couldn't stay away, could he?" she said under her breath.

With a twitch of a smile, Jack shook his head.

When she reached the front of the line, Bill motioned for her to step up to the table. Serena said, "Hello, officer. I'm ready for duty."

His cold steel blue eyes met hers, and Bill said, "It's *detective*."

"Sorry, detective." Serena held out her hand, and he placed it on a glass plate which fit each finger. "I thought you used ink and rolled the finger on paper. Darn."

"We've evolved." Bill gave her the scary look again. "Police carry mobile scanners and can fingerprint anywhere." He paused to check the scan. "Done."

"Do I have permission to leave?" Serena asked politely.

"Here, yes. The room, no."

"O-o-o…kay." Serena searched the room for an empty chair. Most people had taken their seats, except for one by the dresser, Enrique. *Time to make friends.*

Enrique scooted his chair in the opposite direction when Serena sat next to him. "Enrique, right?" She stuck out her hand. "We got off to a bad start, but let's be friends. It might help pass the time."

"Fine." Enrique gave her hand one shake.

"Can I pick your brain?"

"For your book?"

Serena wasn't sure how to answer. "If it was, would you answer?"

"I would."

"You dress models for the show, and from what I've seen, you do a wonderful job."

Enrique shifted in his seat to better see her. "I believe I do."

"You're a perfectionist. I'd choose someone like you, too." Serena hoped he'd let his guard down before she asked heavy hitting questions.

"I label everything," Enrique answered.

This might be easier than I thought. "Even the shoes?"

"Yes, I label the container with a code. Only the model and I know their number. That way, no one can accuse anyone else of taking their things. Makes life easier."

"I didn't know that." *I didn't know that! How could I find the models' shoes and loosen the heels? It's proof I didn't do it.* "Did you tell Detective Ando how you label the shoes?"

"He didn't ask." Enrique folded his arms over his chest. "I'm not giving him any clues which may point him my way."

"I must agree, but if you didn't do it, the information would clear a lot of names."

"Like you?" Enrique closed one eye.

"Well…yes." Serena confessed. "Besides you, only the models know their codes."

Enrique held up his index finger. "Not necessarily. Mia and some of the staff are aware of my system."

"Are you thirsty?" Serena changed to a safe topic. "The bartender has arrived."

"I'll take an iced tea. Thank you."

Serena hoped to run into Jack without Enrique seeing. She chose an indirect route, weaving through tables occupied by models and staff, yet never saw him. The bartender smiled when she approached.

"How can I help you?" he gave her a broad smile.

"Two iced teas, please." Serena watched him expertly prepare them. "Could you accidentally throw a shot of whiskey into mine?" she teased.

"I wish. But I have strict orders." He placed the drinks on the bar. "Anything else?"

"Yes, have we met before?" Serena considered it a safe opening question.

"I work at The Pearl. I'm really the bartender."

"Now it makes sense. I'm Serena, by the way."

"The novelist."

"Thanks for that."

"It's an excellent book."

"Wow. You read." The man appeared to be in his late twenties, and she never dreamed he had read her book or any book for that matter. Serena felt guilty for judging him.

The man chuckled. "I read when I can." He held up his phone. "On this."

"It's a great way when you're on the go. Hey, I didn't catch your name."

"Jonathan."

"I'll get you a signed copy if you'd like. I know the author." Serena winked.

"That's great," Jonathan said in an excited voice.

"Before I go back to my seat, Jonathan, could you do me a favor?"

"Anything."

"Find Jack Ando and ask him to come to my table." Carrying the drinks, Serena returned to the table to discover Enrique engaged in a conversation with the model seated next to him. "Here you go." She slid the drink in front of him.

Serena sipped on her drink and checked out the room. She noticed Natalie, the plus-size model, at a table with other women, but no one spoke to her. Isabella was the center of attention at hers. Teddy wandered the room taking photos, and Serena wondered if he had permission. She scribbled in her notebook as realization struck her. Every single person had a reason to harm Ava. Even the guy next to her. He was a perfectionist, and they didn't like it when someone messed with their system.

"May I have your attention?" Jack asked, positioning himself in the center of the room. "The shoe results are in. They found no extra fingerprints. Only from the model who wore the shoes. This does not clear anyone. The culprit may have worn gloves."

"Ugh." Serena slumped in her chair. "So much for that."

"You called," a male voice whispered in her ear.

"Oh, detective, you startled me," Serena put her hand over her heart. "Did you come to interview us?" She cocked her head towards Enrique.

"Indeed, I did." Jack widened his eyes. "Always looking for fresh evidence."

"Enrique has some interesting facts to tell," Serena replied.

"Did I hear my name?" Enrique spun in his seat to face them. "Oh. Detective, I didn't see you."

"I'd like to ask a few more questions," Jack answered. "Make sure I have every detail."

"Enrique has a detail," Serena said.

"Serena!" Enrique hissed.

"Do tell." Jack put his hands on his hips, and his arm was close enough for Serena to touch the hardened muscle.

Serena sipped her tea as Enrique spilled his to Jack. She made sure he revealed every detail. When the man completed his story, Jack turned to her. "You're off the suspect list."

"Thank you! There's no way I knew about his system, and my girls wouldn't have learned about it until after dress rehearsal. I never returned to the dressing room until after the show."

"You're good at this," Jack said. "Don't let it go to your head." He stared at Serena as if deciding something. "I have enough proof you didn't do this. You can leave now. Go work on your next book."

"Jack, if I may?" Serena pointed to a secluded corner.

Jack followed Serena, and she turned to face him. "I need to stay."

"Oh, no."

"I'll talk to Nina then. She'll approve my request."

"Fine. But sit at the bar. If you leave, you must tell me and report to me when you return."

"Thanks." Serena grinned. "You won't be sorry. I'm a great observer of people."

"Didn't I just say…?"

"Sit at the bar?" Serena gave him an innocent look. "How come we've never met? I've been coming to The Pearl for over a year."

"We've passed by each other."

He noticed me! "We did?"

"Whenever you left the building, I'd check your office. Made sure you locked up and everything was secure."

"That is so sweet."

"No, it's my job."

"Well, thank you."

"You're welcome."

Jack stood so close Serena inhaled his scent. "You're nice," she whispered.

"So are you."

Chapter Eight

After she came back down to earth, Serena pointed to the exit. "I'm going to zip over to my office for a minute. I'll be back shortly and take my place at the bar. Is that okay, Detective?"

"I told you to call me Jack," he answered in what Serena thought was a sultry voice. "You're free to go, Serena, and as I said, you don't need to come back."

"Somehow." Serena tapped her chin. "I decided I like it here, especially since I'm no longer a suspect."

"Ando!" Bill Mitchell bellowed. "A little help here."

"I'll see you later," Serena said, watching Jack stride towards the table. "Now where was I? Office."

Serena waved to Jonathan, the bartender, on her way out. Walking at a brisk pace down the hall, relief spread through her. She was free. A burden lifted from deep inside her. One she didn't realize she carried. *I'll text the girls and let them know.* Her keys jingled like a song in her hand, and she flipped through them, searching for the office key.

Once inside, her eyes went to the wall she'd cleared for her suspect board. A staff member had mounted a corkboard on the wall across from her computer, as requested. Serena ran her hand over it, admiring its look. She turned to her counter and found push pins and yarn. "All set. You get great service here."

Serena reached for the pictures she'd printed. *Do I need to put my picture up there? No, but I need to print a few more.* She sank into her chair and searched for Enrique and the bartender. "Jonathan seems nice, but you never know."

It took longer to find Jonathan, but using The Pearl's directory, she eventually learned his full name, age and how long he'd worked at the hotel. "Jonathan Price, age twenty-nine. I hope you're not involved." She chose his work photo and guided the arrow to the print button.

Serena gathered the pictures and sorted through them, analyzing each person. She rose from her chair and placed Ava Taylor's picture in the center of the board. As she mounted each photo around her, she cut sections of yarn and connected them to Ava with push pins. She took a step back and studied her board.

"There's Isabella, *my* number one suspect, and Ruby, who is a long shot. I have seen nothing that points her way. Next is Natalie, the sweet plus-size model, but I can't rule her out just because I have a soft spot for her. I also have one for Teddy, but I'm holding judgement until I hear the toxicology report. If someone drugged Ava, besides messing with her shoes, he moves to the top of the list. Aurora?" Serena lifted her shoulder. "Who would sabotage their own shoe? That's a longshot."

Serena paced in front of the board. "I'm ruling out Savannah. I haven't seen or heard any stories about her." She stopped in front of the board. "I'm saving the best for last. You, Enrique. You told me an interesting story, and your face twitched when you spoke about the murder. Was that a sign?" She touched Jonathan's picture. "I'm coming back to watch you but please don't be guilty. I like you."

Before leaving, Serena snapped a picture of the board. When she collected more evidence, she'd call a P.I.C. meeting. She imagined Mia was cleaning up the mess which had spread all over social media, and Lily was studying the footage. They needed time to work.

Serena sent a text to her daughters to update them on the situation. She finished with: *Even though I'm free to go, I'm staying. I want to see this through to the end. Ask Grandma to stay until I come home. Love to you all.* Serena added a few hugs and kisses after the message.

When Serena returned to the bar, the staff had set up a buffet along one wall. She wandered over to check out the food since she hadn't eaten since breakfast. *What time is it?* Well past dinnertime according to her watch and inching toward her bedtime hour.

After filling her plate, Serena headed for the last seat at the bar. She promised to stay out of the way and would keep her pledge. As she nibbled on a carrot, an iced tea slid in front of her.

"Your drink of choice?" Jonathan asked.

"Thanks. Anything good happen while I've been away?" Serena placed the carrot on her plate.

"Mostly interviews. The police have sent some people to their rooms."

"I see our favorite detective, Bill Mitchell, is still here."

"He's something…and demanding. I had to mix cranberry juice and soda just the right way. If he didn't like it, he made me do it over."

"What a waste of cranberry," Serena said. "Next time, give the one he doesn't like to me."

"You sound like Jack. He said the same thing."

Two peas in a pod. Serena smiled. "Do you know Jack?"

"Of course. I've worked here for seven years. Jack is part of The Pearl's security team."

"That's right." *Now's my chance to discover more about him.* "Does he have a favorite drink?"

"Jack doesn't drink much, but when he does, he has a beer."

"Does he ever sit at the bar, like I am, and talk to you? People like to spill their inner thoughts to the bartender." Serena winked.

"No, Jack keeps to himself, but he's a stand-up guy. He'll solve this case quickly."

"Not before I do."

"What did you say?" Jonathan asked. He'd taken care of guests while they chatted and just finished an order.

"I said, 'I hope so, too.'"

"Yeah, although I don't mind the extra attention I'm getting from the models." Jonathan lifted his brows. "It's been fun. Well, mostly before the murder happened."

"They're flirting with you?" Serena asked. "You *are* cute." *Typical blonde surfer boy.*

"Thanks." Jonathan's cheeks flushed pink. "Some models flirt more than others."

"Ooh, do tell."

"Here comes one now."

Serena glanced over her shoulder to find her nemesis approaching. "Hello, Isabella. Have you heard I'm not a suspect anymore?"

Isabella rolled her eyes. "Whatever." She turned her attention to Jonathan. "Hey, care to give a girl a drink?"

"The usual?"

"Absolutely."

"Is it code for putting that brand of vodka in your drink?" Serena asked, as Jonathan handed Isabella a tomato juice.

Isabella stared at Serena for a moment, tossed her head and walked away.

"Isabella doesn't have manners," Serena said to Jonathan. "She didn't say thank you."

"I'm used to it," Jonathan answered with a shrug. "But she's a good tipper. She had me bring champagne to the dressing room during rehearsals and the morning of the show."

"Really?" Serena flipped open her journal and wrote the details she'd learned. "Did she share or was it just for her?"

"Isabella is not the sharing type," Jonathan answered. "Neither was Ava. I had to separately deliver their orders."

We seamlessly moved on to Ava. Now I can ask about her. "Ava was quite the beauty. Before this happened did you consider asking her out?" Serena kept her eyes on the page.

"No." Jonathan sounded dejected. "Before I could even explore the possibility, Ava reminded me I was just the bartender. As if she knew I'd ask."

Also, a reason to drug her. Not to kill her but to make her more agreeable or get revenge? He might enjoy seeing her stumble on the stage. I'm sure Jonathan can get drugs. No! I hope it's not true.

"Serena? Are you okay?" Jonathan asked as he refilled her glass.

"Yes, I'm fine. It's been a long day."

"While you were gone, Detective Mitchell announced everyone could leave at nine p.m. The ones who are still suspects must report back tomorrow at ten a.m."

Busy talking with Jonathan and taking notes, Serena hardly noticed the dwindling crowd. Most people seated at the tables were part of her board, except for one potential suspect who had departed. *Enrique? They let him go?*

The room had cleared out by nine o'clock. Bill Mitchell had packed up and left before the hour. Only Serena, Jack and Jonathan remained. Jack walked toward them, rubbing the spot between his eyes. "Hey, Jonathan, I could use a beer," he said.

"Coming right up."

"Thanks, buddy. You can leave, too."

"Sure thing."

"Hi," Serena said. "You look tired."

"I am, but do you have time to talk?"

Her heart raced at the invitation. "Yes, I have time. Nina sent me a room key. I'm staying overnight." *Why did I say that? Good thing I didn't blurt out my room number.*

"The tox screen won't be ready until tomorrow. Hopefully, we'll get more answers."

"Is the screen reliable?"

"It's a preliminary test, but yes. If only one or two drugs show up, it can be ready in twenty-four to forty-eight hours. Alcohol content takes less time. We also do a full toxicology test, which takes four to six weeks."

"Why let Enrique go?" Serena asked. "Just curious."

"Enrique may be a perfectionist, but he's an equal opportunist when speaking about the models. They all get on his nerves. Everyone is incapable of doing things the correct way, except for him. He didn't have any grudges or attitude toward anyone." Jack glanced away.

"What?" Serena tapped his arm. "Tell me."

"Except for you." Jack lifted the corner of his mouth. "You caused him a bit of anxiety." He chuckled.

"It's not funny," Serena said. She thought for a moment and recalled their first meeting. *Helicopter parent coming in for a landing. I hovered and spoke for my girls.* "Okay, it's a little funny." She giggled and sent a silent promise. *Girls, I'm sorry. I'll do better.*

"How are your girls?" Jack asked. "Did you let them know you're not a suspect anymore?"

I could fall in love with you, Jack Ando. You asked about the girls. "I texted them from my office. I haven't checked my phone to see if they responded. It usually takes them a while."

"What are you waiting for?" Jack pointed to her phone lying next to her notebook. "I bet they're elated."

Serena discovered four messages, two from each daughter. *Yay!!!!* Jade had written. The next one was a GIF of a dancing dog, which she showed Jack.

"Cute." Jack smiled.

Jewel, the more sensitive child, sent, *Happy tears. I love you, Mom. You're the best.* Her GIF showed two cartoon bears hugging each other with a caption which said, "Sending hugs." She turned her phone so Jack could see.

"Are they okay?" Jack asked. "They've gone through a traumatic experience today."

"My mom is a sympathetic listener," Serena answered. "When I get home, I'll double and triple check them."

"Your ex didn't stay with them?"

Serena blew through her lips.

"That's a statement." Jack chuckled.

"It's the first we've seen of him since Christmas. Birthdays and Christmas. Those are his main events."

"You don't share custody?" Jack wrinkled his brow.

"Yes, he can see them whenever he wants. He chooses…"

"Christmas and birthdays." Jack took a sip of beer. "If it were me, I'd see them as much as I could."

"You don't have kids, I take it," Serena said, although she knew the answer.

"No, I'd hoped to, but it didn't work out."

"Sorry."

"Don't be." Jack moved the beer bottle between his hands. "Do you mind if I ask a personal question?"

"Nope. I'm an open book." Serena pressed her lips together. "Get it? Open book."

"Yeah, I got it. You wrote a book." The twitch of a smile showed for an instant. "Did you invite Justice to the show?"

"My goodness, no. According to him, the girls texted him."

"Okay, makes sense. Now that they're older, they can stay in contact through texts," Jack said. "That's a good thing, right?"

"Maybe. When I called Justice to thank him for the flowers, he said that's how they communicated."

"Wait." Jack pointed the bottle at her. "This sounds serious. Justice sent you flowers?"

"To congratulate me on my book. I haven't heard from him since Christmas." Serena studied the man. "Are you jealous?"

"Me?" Jack stuck a thumb in his chest. "No. I barely know you."

"You know enough." Serena paused. "Justice only sent the flowers because he heard of my success. He didn't send them to the old Serena Tate. He sent them to the successful author with an office at The Pearl hotel. I never got flowers from him before."

"Oh?" Jack appeared to relax. "Don't let him take advantage of you, Serena."

"Never." *Don't tell him we kissed. I almost fell for Justice's charm again.* "Well, it's been nice chatting. I'm going up to my room."

"I'll see you tomorrow."

"Same place, same bar stool," Serena said, longing to kiss him. She got down from the chair, leaning towards him. "Good night." Serena inhaled his scent one last time.

"Good night."

Chapter Nine

Serena called for a nine a.m. P.I.C. meeting, and everyone showed up on time. "Thanks for coming," she said. "Did you get the photo I sent last night?"

"Yes," Lily answered. "You've been busy."

"And so have you two," Serena answered. "Mia, any luck putting out the fires?"

"No." Mia hung her head. "One of the world's supermodels dies at your show. What do I say? Kade said it will blow over, but I want to fix things."

"When it's the right time, you can do a charity show in Ava's honor," Lily said. "I'd be glad to help."

"So would I," Serena replied. "Start a scholarship in her name, too. If you can't get models to walk in the show, my girls would love the opportunity."

"What would I do without you guys?" Mia asked through tears. "Those are great ideas and you've helped. Let's shift our focus from the future and concentrate on the current moment. Serena, you did a great job on your suspect board."

"Thanks, Mia. I have had an update since I sent the photo. Jack has eliminated one of them," Serena replied. "Take Enrique off the board."

"I never thought he did it," Mia said. "He's too nervous and in his own little world of fashion. Don't get me wrong, I love the man, and he's been part of my staff for over a year. I couldn't picture him sabotaging the shoes. He holds fashion in high regard."

"Okay, so he's off the list." Lily studied her phone screen. "None of these people entered the dressing room, except for regular hours. I wasn't any help."

"Don't say that, Lily," Serena said. "You did your job and checked the footage."

Lily looked up from her phone. "Who do you think did it?"

Serena cringed. "I was positive it was Isabella, but I want to see what the tox screen report says."

"You think drugs were involved?" Mia asked. "Models are around many people."

"So are bartenders," Serena answered. "And your photographer was in drug rehab."

"Teddy?"

"Yep. The one and only."

"Well, that narrows it down," Lily said in a sarcastic voice. "We need more information before we continue. When will Jack get the report?"

"Today," Serena replied.

"Mia?" Lily looked at her. "Can you get Jack to reveal the contents of the report?"

"Oh, don't worry," Serena said. "I've got that covered."

* * * *

Serena strolled into the bar and discovered less than half the people from yesterday. She did a quick count. *Eighteen.* Her eyes landed on Natalie, leaning against the farthest wall, looking quite dejected. *Is she crying? I better check on her.*

"Natalie?" Serena held out her arms, wanting to give her a comforting hug.

"Don't." Natalie held up her hand like a stop sign. "Sorry, I didn't mean for that to come out so harsh. If you hugged me, I'd fall to pieces."

Serena gestured to the closest empty table. "Care to share?"

Natalie lifted her shoulder. "There's not much to say." She followed Serena and sat two chairs away. "This is going to sound selfish, Serena. I shouldn't even tell you."

"Then say nothing. I'll sit here until you feel better."

Natalie sniffed and wiped her eyes with a tissue. A few minutes later, she spoke with a quivering voice, "This show marked my debut as a model. Ms. Takeda gave me an opportunity no one else had. Now I'll be associated with Ava's death walk for the rest of my career."

"What? Who calls it that?" *Mia can't find out. How do I keep it from her? The first chance I get, I'm texting Lily.*

"One of the models. I don't know who, but it's spread like wildfire. They can't wait to leave and return to New York."

"We need to stop this," Serena said.

"We?" Natalie shook her head. "I'm staying out of it. Most of them don't talk to me anyway. Ava thought I didn't deserve the job, and Isabella constantly sneers at me."

"Thanks for the information. Anything else I can do for you?"

"No, I'm good," Natalie answered. "You've been so kind to me, Serena. I should thank *you*."

"If you need me, I'll be right over there at the bar." Serena headed for her usual spot, but Jack's appearance stopped her.

His face said it all. Jack had the report. Serena titled her head toward an isolated table with dim lighting. She changed direction and picked a seat where she could see the room.

Jack slid next to her and said, "I shouldn't be surprised, but they found drugs in Ava's system."

"The bartender told me he always delivered champagne to her," Serena said. "Easy to put drugs in her drink."

"Her alcohol level was point zero three, which is low. Not enough to impair her judgement. Alter it, maybe. It wouldn't cause her to lose her balance, either."

"What drug did they discover?"

"An overdose of a powerful sleeping pill. Mixed with the alcohol, it could be lethal."

"Any signs of bruising around her head? Ava dropped onto the stage like a rag doll." Serena slapped her hands on the table. "She may have hit her head."

"No significant signs that she did." Jack waved the manila folder in his hand. "I believe someone wanted her dead."

"Or they wanted Ava to fall and remove her from the show."

"Regardless, it's now a murder case." Jack squeezed Serena's hand. "I need to get back to work."

"Yes. Sure. Go." Serena rubbed her forehead. "This has gone from bad to worse." She dashed off a text to Lily, sharing the news about the tox screen and the model's name for the show. The next text went to Mia, minus the name.

Within seconds, Lily wrote back: *I'm coming. We need to stop this!*

Serena debated whether she should stay at the table instead of heading to her place at the bar. No one would overhear their conversation if she didn't change seats. Before deciding, Lily appeared at the doorway. Serena raised her hand and waved.

Just as Lily reached the table, Jack intervened. "Lily, you can't…"

"Oh, yes, I can, Jack. Sit." Lily pointed to an empty chair.

Serena had forgotten that Lily knew Jack quite well. She didn't know every detail, but they'd worked together in the past. Besides, if he didn't comply, Lily would pull the Nina card. It always worked.

"Is something happening that I'm not aware of?" Jack inquired. "Does it relate to the murder?"

"Murder?" Lily raised her brows.

"Yes," Jack hissed.

"No, it doesn't." Lily made a face at him. "But it's just as important."

"May I?" Serena asked.

"Certainly," Jack said, pursing his lips. "I couldn't stop you if I tried."

Serena bit her lip, took a breath and said, "Natalie told me the models are referring to this weekend as Ava's death walk. This can't get leaked to social media."

"What the…?" Jack rubbed the spot between his eyes.

"Do you do that when you're frustrated, Jack?" Serena asked, gesturing to the spot between her eyes.

"Maybe? I don't know." Jack placed his hands on the table. "Go on. How can I help Mia?"

"When can the models and staff leave?" Lily asked.

"The ones we cleared can leave tomorrow morning."

"Great, it gives us time." Lily faced Serena. "We'd like to address the situation with all the models and staff, right?"

"Yes, we'll…" Serena had no clue. "What will we do, Lily?"

"Don't worry." Lily grinned. "I know how to make a threat without it sounding like one. Jack, can you call a meeting for tonight?"

"Yes, I will, but I need to start my interviews."

"I heard you've got new information," Lily said.

"How…?" Jack shook his head and walked away.

"I've got to scour the web," Lily said. "Look for any signs of Ava's death walk. I doubt anyone here is foolish enough to post while in the hotel, but if they did, I'll suspend their account."

"Wow! You can do that?" Serena looked at Lily in amazement.

"Absolutely. I plan to start as soon as I leave."

"Then let's not waste time," Serena replied. "I'll walk you to the door and take my place at the bar."

* * * *

"Prescription sleeping pills aren't the same as hard drugs, right?" Serena asked Jonathan, wanting to see his reaction.

"Perhaps, but consuming too many can be fatal. Why do you ask?"

"Research for my new book."

"You finally started." Jonathan nodded. "Good to hear."

Serena drummed her fingers on the bar. "Jonathan, we're friends, don't you agree?"

"Yeah." Jonathan stopped to take some drink orders and returned with an iced tea for Serena. "Sorry for the interruption."

"I understand. Work comes first." Serena met his eyes. "If you kept information from the police about Ava or any of the models, would you confide in me?"

"Like what?"

"Shady happenings." Serena held up her glass. "Spill the tea."

"I told the officers everything, but let me think about it," Jonathan replied as he moved to the far end of the bar to take an order.

Serena spun on her stool and watched Jack interview Natalie. *Is he informing them about Ava's murder? He never announced it to the room. Was there a reason not to reveal the recent evidence? Use it for shock value? Ooh, he's done. Natalie is heading this way and appears to need a motherly hug.*

"Serena." Natalie stopped in front of her.

Serena hopped from the stool and barely hugged her before the woman pulled away. "Remember what I told you?" Natalie asked.

"You'll burst into tears if someone comforts you," Serena replied. "Maybe it's what you need to do."

"No, I must remain in control. Everyone is your enemy. The girls are backstabbing each other. Even the ones the police deemed innocent, and it's quite ugly."

"When did this happen? Not here." Serena checked for the location of her journal and spotted it at the corner of the bar. *Time to add more observations to you.*

"Last night in the hotel hallway. We're all on the same floor."

"Can I ask you a favor?" Serena took the model's hand. "Please keep me informed. You don't deserve hate. Look at me. We're almost the same size."

"No." Natalie shook her head. "You're definitely smaller than me."

"Thanks for the compliment," Serena said, grinning like the Cheshire cat. "I'll take it." She changed her expression to one of concern when she saw how upset Natalie was. "Really, Natalie. I want to help."

"Thanks, Serena, but I don't think there's anything you can do," Natalie answered as she returned to her table.

* * * *

"You're letting Isabella leave?" Serena tried to process what Jack had told her. When she saw Isabella head for the exit, Serena had hopped off her stool and headed straight for Jack.

"Yes. No evidence points in her direction." Jack let out a breath. "She doesn't drink or do drugs. Isabella is a vegan. Her body is a temple."

"You fell for that line?" Serena closed one eye. "The temple thing."

"Whatever." Jack smirked. "I'm focused on the drugs, and she doesn't fit the profile."

"She could easily get her hands on any drug she wanted."

"Isabella was truthful about it. She said the same thing."

"What about the shoes?" Serena asked. "Do you think two crimes were committed? Someone sabotaged the shoes, and another person drugged Ava."

"Not sure yet. Anyone can get sleeping pills, but someone familiar with drugs might know the correct dosage."

"Like Teddy?" Serena cringed.

"So, you know." Jack smiled at her, a real smile. "You're invested in this, aren't you?"

"Darn right I am. My girls were part of the show. What if Ava offered them champagne without me knowing? Have you tested the contents of the bottle?"

"Since there was more than one bottle, we're checking each one. Bill is at the station helping with the tests."

"I wondered where he was," Serena said. "Did you arrange for him to be in charge of the champagne bottles?"

"Yes, I did."

"I knew I liked you." Serena paused, hoping for a similar response. When she couldn't stand the silence, she said, "I'm going for a walk. I'll come back in an hour."

"Gardens?"

Serena nodded.

"I wish I could come. It's a great place to clear your head."

"When this is over, we'll take a walk," Serena replied. She focused on the exit and refrained from glancing back. If Jack answered, she never heard.

Arriving at the pond, Serena watched the koi swim without checking for Sam. The oval-shaped pool was at least twenty feet long, so he could be anywhere. She walked to a bench and opened her purse. Inside, she'd stored a bag of honey nut oats for Sam and the other fish. As if they could smell the food, Sam and three others emerged from the water.

"Is that your family, Sam? Wife and two kids." Serena stood and walked to the white Japanese-style railing which surrounded the pond. "Here you go." She tossed a handful into the water.

Once fed, the others swam away, but Sam stayed. "Sam," Serena said with a sigh. "Jack let my number one suspect go. I understand why, but I still think she did it.

Jade told me Ava and Isabella fought all the time." She looked upward. "But is that enough to accuse her?"

Serena heard a splash and checked on Sam. "You don't think she did it, do you? Are you shaking your head? Okay. Then who? Teddy?" She returned to the bench and sank onto it. "Oh, my, gosh. That's it. Jack knows about Teddy's drug use and thinks he did it. Can I prove him wrong?"

Sam swam in circles, and Serena couldn't figure out the meaning. "Am I right, Sam? Do I clear Teddy's name?"

Sam opened and closed his mouth, staring at Serena.

"You agree, I can tell." Serena pointed at the fish. "I'm going to have a cup of tea, Sam. It may help me focus on what to do next."

Chapter Ten

Serena looked up from her phone to discover Lily sitting at her table. "Well?" Lily asked. "You look deep in thought."

"I am." Serena pushed an empty teacup towards Lily. "Jack let Isabella go. I think he suspects Teddy."

"Teddy, the nervous photographer."

"Right."

"If I recall." Lily cocked her head. "He had a drug problem and told you Ava always harassed him. It makes sense. He's got motive and knows how to get his hands on drugs."

"The culprit used a powerful sleeping pill. Anyone can get those," Serena answered. "They could have a family member who uses them."

"I see your point." Lily added a spoonful of sugar to her tea. "Where do we begin?"

"First, I'll casually interview Teddy when I return to the bar. Only his friends can call him Teddy, you know," Serena teased.

"That happened fast," Lily said with a chuckle. "I guess he's Ted to me from now on."

"Have you met him?" Serena asked.

"I saw him rushing around the venue, but I never got a formal introduction."

"From what I've learned, he got clean, and the fashion world obviously took him back. Why would he ruin his career over one model?"

"This model could damage his career, Serena."

Serena shook her head. "Mia hired him and knows Ava harassed him."

"Does she?" Lily raised her brows.

"I'll double check." Serena dashed off a text.

"Speaking of Mia," Lily said. "We need to protect her reputation at all costs. I'll see you at seven tonight. You introduce me, emphasizing my tech skills. I'll take it from there."

"Can we be a little threatening?" Serena asked. "Some models are still throwing shade at each other. Natalie told me how they're backstabbing anyone they think is guilty."

"Only Natalie? Did someone confirm her story?"

"Come to think of it…no." Serena poured another cup of tea. "I'll check into it." Staring at her favorite picture, the marumado, Serena concentrated on the one lone pink flower on the branch. "I believe one person committed the crime, not two."

"Is Jack leaning towards two?"

"I think so. It's hard to tell with him."

Lily held her teacup in the air. "Serena?" She closed one eye. "I just realized you have a crush on Jack. Do you?"

"No." Serena fumbled with her silverware. "Where are those tea sandwiches? I ordered the cucumber ones with cream cheese. There's enough to share."

"You're avoiding the question." Lily giggled. "You're guilty as charged."

"Stop." Serena giggled with Lily. "I'm a forty-something woman with two teens about to become adults. I don't have crushes."

"You deserve to have a little fun, Serena. As you said, your girls have grown up. You dedicated all your time to them since the divorce. I bet they'd be the first ones to say, 'Go for it.'"

Serena blew through her lips. "I can't tell if he likes me, Lily. Every time we have a moment…" She lifted her hand. "Poof. It's gone."

"Jack is in the middle of a criminal investigation," Lily said. "In everyday life, he's a hard person to read so during a case, it's worse. When I come tonight, I'll watch how he interacts with you."

"You know him better than I do," Serena replied. "But don't you dare give anything away." Her phone pinged. "It's Mia. She's asking if we're having a meeting without her. What do I say?"

"You came for a break, and we met by chance. Did she answer your question?"

"Yes." Serena nodded. "She knows, but also asked if it makes Teddy guilty."

✳ ✳ ✳ ✳

"I'd like to start by asking everyone to please be seated," Jack addressed the audience. He waited for the noise to stop and continued. "Most are welcome to leave the hotel tomorrow but check in with me first. Departure time begins at twelve noon."

Protests filled the air, and Jack placed his hand on his hip. "Or maybe you'd like to stay?" Silence took over the room. "Fine. Noon it is." He turned to Serena and swept his hand toward her. "Serena would like to speak with you now."

"Thank you, Jack. It's come to my attention that someone started a horrible rumor. I'm sure it's not true and no one here would want to hurt Mia Takeda's standing in the fashion world." Serena took a cleansing breath. "I've heard someone labeled this weekend Ava's Death Walk."

Gasps came from the crowd, and people talked amongst themselves.

Serena cleared her throat. "To make sure we don't ruin anyone's reputation, Ms. Takeda's or any of yours, I've invited Lily Nichols to speak with you." She looked over at her friend. "You have the floor."

"Thank you, Serena." Lily stepped forward. "Hello, everyone, I'd like to provide some information about who I am. I'm employed at Nicholworks. You may be familiar with the company. It is a creative tech firm, but I am the person behind security and the nuts and bolts of keeping it up and running. Yeah, it's makes me a tech nerd."

"You're too beautiful to be a nerd," a man said from the audience.

"Thanks, but that's not why we're here." Lily paused. "I will scan the web daily for any mention of Ava or the death walk. If I find one word, I will hunt you down. Post anything on social media, I'll shut down your accounts, and you won't get them back. If you talk to a reporter, and I discover someone passed this disgusting rumor along to the press, it might be difficult to find work."

"Are you threatening us?" a woman shouted from a table in the back corner.

"Not at all. It's a free country. Do as you wish. I like to be honest and upfront. That's why I'm telling you to think before you step foot outside of this hotel. Mia Takeda had nothing to do with Ava's death. In this day of social media, we know how quickly rumors, gossip and even the truth can spread. Yes, she is my friend. Whatever it takes, I will protect her. Sadly, this is why we called the meeting. It's not related to Ava's passing but linked to what lies ahead. I hope in your hearts you see the truth and agree with me." Lily held out her hands. "That's it. You're free to go unless Jack wants to say anything."

"You said it all, Lily," Jack answered. "I agree. Enough destruction has happened. Let's end it here."

A group of people headed for the exit, whispering as they made their way to the door. Serena went to her barstool, checking for Teddy. She hadn't seen him leave so she scanned the room for any sign of him. When their eyes met, she waved him over. "Care for a drink before we call it a night?" she asked.

"If it's non-alcohol, yes," Teddy answered.

Serena got Jonathan's attention. "I'll have the usual," she said.

"Club soda," Teddy added.

"How are you holding up, Teddy?" Serena asked. "Did Detective Ando tell you about the drugs found in Ava's system?"

"Yes," Teddy replied. "I think he saved it for his individual questioning for shock value."

Serena nodded. "To get a reaction."

"Exactly."

Jonathan slid two glasses in front of them. "Enjoy," he said with a wink.

"I'm not…" Serena pointed to her chest, then to Teddy. "No…oh, never mind."

"I'm glad we found time to talk," Teddy said. "There's something I wanted to ask you."

"Fire away."

"The day we met I told you Ava criticized my photography. Did you tell anyone else the story, like Detective Ando?"

"No," Serena answered. *Wait a minute. Teddy appears concerned, almost scared.* "Do you want me to tell him?"

Teddy vigorously shook his head. "You don't need to share our personal conversation. Besides, I told him Ava and I never got along."

"I believe it was more than that. You worried she could get you fired."

"Did I say that?"

Serena couldn't remember his exact words. "I can't recall."

"Serena?" Lily touched her shoulder, and Serena spun on the stool to face her. "Would you like to join us at the rooftop bar for a nightcap? Mia and Kade are already there." She held up her phone. "Gabe just texted me."

"Thanks for the invite, but I'm exhausted. I'd love to sleep for one hundred hours. Tell everyone I said hi and thanks for including me," Serena answered.

"I'll talk to you in the morning," Lily said. "Let's have tea. Start the day right."

"Okay, I'll be there at eight a.m. It gives me an hour before I come here." Serena turned back to Teddy. "Sorry you don't get to leave with the masses, but I'll be here to keep you company." She gestured to Lily. "We plan to prove you're innocent."

Teddy's eyes widened, yet he said nothing.

"Teddy? Did you hear me?"

"Yeah." Teddy jumped off his barstool. "I got to go. I just remembered something."

* * * *

"Serena? Can you hear me?"

Yes, Jack, I heard you. If this is a dream, don't wake me.

A warm hand wrapped around Serena's shoulder, and her body shook. "Come on. Open your eyes."

I'm dreaming about Jack and refuse to wake up. Now where was I? Candlelit dinner, holding hands across the table.

"Get some water," Jack said.

What? No. I'll take another glass of champagne.

A cool liquid hit Serena's face. *Who did that?* "What the heck?" she yelled, waving her hand for it to stop.

"Thank goodness." Lily's voice floated into her dream.

It's not a dream. Why would Lily throw water in my face? Serena struggled to open her eyes. "Lily?" Another face came into view. "Jack?"

"You weren't kidding when you said you wanted to sleep for one hundred hours." Lily chuckled.

"I believe they drugged her with the same sleeping pill used on Ava," Jack grumbled. "We might have found our killer." He looked into Serena's eyes. "Are you willing to take a blood test?"

"Jack," Lily snapped. "She's barely awake. Give the woman time to process."

"Who would drug me?" Serena mumbled.

"Ted Lewis. The person who sat next to you all night," Jack answered.

"That's right! Serena turned her back on him to speak with me," Lily said. "He had time to slip something into her drink."

"But we think he's innocent, Lily," Serena whispered.

"Not anymore, my friend. Why did he spike your drink if he was?" Lily huffed.

"Think, Serena," Jack said, taking her hand. "What did you talk about last night? Did he accidentally give you incriminating information, then realize what he'd done?"

Serena fought to remember. "Teddy asked if I told you something. I said I hadn't."

"What was it?"

"Let her wake up, Jack," Lily said. "She can't think clearly yet."

"What time is it?" Serena asked, coming to her senses. "How did you get in here?"

"It's nine-thirty," Lily answered. "Jack is Pearl security. He can get in any room he wants. When you didn't come for tea, I knew something was wrong. I gave you an extra half hour to show in case I was mistaken. Then I texted Jack. He came to the tearoom, and we decided to check on you." She slipped her hand into Serena's. "How do you feel, Serena?"

"Groggy. A shower might help." Serena threw back the comforter and realized she only wore a long t-shirt.

"I'll help her, Jack," Lily said. "You wait in the living area. We'll be out soon."

"I've ordered some hot coffee and have an officer on their way." Jack walked to the bedroom entrance and turned back. "Also, there's an APB on Ted Lewis. No one can find him. Seems like he's disappeared."

"With The Pearl's security team and the police department looking for him, I'm sure you will," Lily said, helping Serena walk to the bathroom. Once Jack left the room, she shook her head. "I thought you were right about Ted, Serena. Let's hope the shower helps you recall the missing piece we need."

"Did Jack say APB?" Serena wrinkled her brow. "There's no need to send an all-points bulletin on me. I'm standing right here."

"Shower." Lily pointed to the bathroom. "Call if you need me."

In the shower, Serena's memory gradually came back to her. She recalled her first conversation with Teddy, and the one last night.

"No, Teddy!" She slapped the shower's wall, turned off the water and grabbed a towel, saying under her breath, "Not so fast. He might be innocent. I need to take a blood test. The drugs may not match."

Serena dressed in the lavender blouse and skinny jeans Lily had placed on the counter. She'd pulled her hair into a ballerina bun yesterday, and despite the long sleep, it had stayed in place. *I must not have moved.* She smoothed down the front part of her hair and applied a pink gloss to her lips. Her mouth felt like someone stuffed twenty cotton balls in it. *Hope the coffee is ready.*

Opening the door, Serena discovered Lily leaning against the wall across from the bathroom. "Lily, you startled me!"

"Sorry. I wanted to be close by if you needed me. Remember anything?"

"Yes, but first I need coffee."

Chapter Eleven

A woman wearing a police uniform and latex gloves greeted Serena and handed her a water bottle. "Drink. I have a feeling you need to hydrate before I take the blood sample."

"Thanks." Serena chugged down the cool water, taking a few breaths in between. "You were right. I needed that," she replied after finishing the bottle.

"Good news," Lily said to Jack. "Serena remembers what happened."

"Great." Jack stood and gestured for Serena to join him on the sofa. "Coffee's ready."

The table in front of the couch held a tray filled with cups, sugar, creamer and a coffee pot. Jack poured the steaming liquid into a mug and said, "How do you like it?"

Serena melted inside. No one ever prepared her coffee before. *How do I like it? I'll tell you how I'd like it.* "Two sugars and a splash of cream," she answered. "Ooh, a little more. There you go." Jack placed the cup on the table and waited for Serena to sit.

"Jack, you're such a gentleman," Serena said. She sipped the coffee. "Perfection."

"I'm glad you like it," Jack replied. "Now, on to business. Officer Downing is also a nurse. She'd prefer to draw your blood in a few minutes, after the water takes effect. You can speak freely in front of her."

Serena nodded and retold the story from the day she'd met Ted Lewis. "He said no one liked Ava Taylor, and she always criticized his work. When Ava approached us, Teddy acted like a scared rabbit. She wasn't kind to him and insinuated that Mia hired him because she couldn't get this other photographer. I can't recall his name."

"That doesn't matter," Jack said. "Ready for the test?"

"Sure." Serena winced when Officer Downing jabbed her skin and didn't look while she drew the blood.

"There," the woman said. "Finished." She applied a bandage and patted Serena's arm. "That's all I need. I'll get this to the lab, Jack, and call you when I get the results."

"Thanks, Sue." Jack waited until the officer left. "I think we should order food. Can you eat something, Serena?"

"A bagel with cream cheese," Serena answered.

"I'll call the kitchen," Lily said as a knock came at the door. "Did the officer forget something?" She opened to discover an angry Mia on the other side.

Mia pushed past Lily and into the sitting area. Folding her arms across her chest, she yelled, "What's going on here, and why wasn't I included?"

"I'll explain," Lily said, "After I call room service. Bagel?"

"What?" Mia had balled her hands into fists, but now they slowly relaxed. "Cinnamon with butter." She turned to face Serena. "You seem tired, Serena. Are you okay?"

"Fine." Serena held up her coffee mug. "A little of this, and I'll be good as new."

Lily returned from placing the order and said, "We didn't have time to call you, Mia. Sorry. Everything happened so fast."

"Start from the beginning," Mia replied and sank into a chair as they each told their part of the story. "Ted Lewis is guilty?" she asked. "I can't believe he's capable of pulling off the crime. However, if a person is angry or worried about their livelihood, they might summon the courage to inflict harm." She covered her face with her hand. "Still. Teddy?"

"I had a blood test, Mia," Serena said. "The results may not match the drug that killed Ava."

"Or he has a variety of sleeping pills," Jack stated. "Ted also made a run for it. Would an innocent man do that?" His phone rang, and he answered, "Jack Ando here."

Silence prevailed as the group waited for the conversation to end. Serena watched her friends' faces and could tell Mia was still hurt. At that moment in time, Lily had made the right choice and contacted Jack. *I'll make sure Mia understands.* She reached for her phone and sent Lily and Mia the P.I.C. message. When they received the text, they nodded.

Jack ended his call and addressed the women. "That was Bill Mitchell. They got Ted Lewis. Found him at the airport. He'd booked a flight to Mexico."

"Where is he now?" Serena asked.

"Lockup."

Serena had no words. Her heart broke, and she chastised herself for letting personal feelings impede an investigation. At first, she befriended people to help write her story and looked upon the crime as material for her book. Yet the more she got involved, she liked the detective side of it. "Everyone, if you don't mind, I'd like to be alone," she said.

"Of course," Mia replied. "Why don't we meet in the tearoom at eleven?"

Serena checked her watch. *Forty-five minutes should give me enough time.* "Yes, I'll see you there."

* * * *

Once Jack, Lily and Mia left her suite, Serena hopped from the sofa and gathered her things. "I need to go to my office." She cracked the door open to see if the coast was clear, then sprinted to the elevator. "What am I doing? No one can see me."

Stopping at the lobby level, Serena zoomed around the corner, still wanting to remain hidden. *There are cameras everywhere. Jack is probably watching me make a fool of myself.* Serena smiled as she unlocked her door, recalling how sweetly he had treated her this morning.

Everything in the office was in its rightful place. Serena turned toward her board, took off the scarf she'd pinned over it and studied her suspects. "I guess I need to take you all down," she told the pictures. "Except you, Teddy."

Her hand froze midair like someone was trying to stop her. Serena stared at the photos. "No. I'm only taking some of you down." She unpinned Ruby, Savannah and Aurora. "I found no evidence to convict you, and neither did Jack."

To her surprise, it left three people pinned to the board. Jonathan, the bartender. Natalie, the plus-size model, and Teddy, the photographer. She liked them all. She touched Jonathan's photo, then Natalie's. "To free Teddy, I'd have to prove one of you committed the crime. This is messy." Serena checked the hour. "I still have time to speak with someone who might help me."

Serena grabbed her handbag and notebook, locked her office and took the quickest route to the gardens. The office hallway came out by the front desk and hotel entrance, so she went through the red Torii gate. She heard the koi pond fountain before she even arrived. *Sam, please be there.*

The fish didn't disappoint. When Serena leaned on the railing, he surfaced from the pond. "Hello, Samurai." She threw him some honey nut oat snacks. "I need your opinion. The police arrested Teddy. I still don't think he did it. Should I pursue my quest to prove him innocent or accept his guilt?"

Sam splashed his tail and held his body up. Serena noticed his white underbelly that traveled up each side. "I learn something new about you every time I visit." She tossed a few more oat snacks. "Let's try this. Heads, I keep looking for the actual killer. Tails, I stop." *Am I crazy talking to a fish and expecting him to answer?*

The koi swam in circles, then popped up his head.

"Heads. I got my answer." Serena pointed at him. "Which means I must look at Jonathan and Natalie." She tapped her chin. "I need to keep an open mind. Just because I took someone off the board doesn't mean they're innocent. Thanks for the help. It's tearoom time."

Serena walked along the flagstone path, feeling like herself again. The grogginess had worn off, and the day appeared clearer and brighter. She'd found time to text the twins but didn't tell them someone drugged her. She asked about their day and discovered Justice had taken them to dinner. He even asked how Serena was surviving. *That was nice. Stop. It's one dinner and one concerning question about me. Plus, he never made me coffee.*

Stepping into the tearoom helped a person escape from the everyday rush, and Serena couldn't wait for the feeling to overtake her. She inhaled the jasmine scent that greeted her at the door. When they spotted Serena, Lily and Mia waved from their designated table in the back corner. The moss-colored walls seemed to engulf her in a warm hug as she walked toward them.

"I needed this," Serena said, sitting by Mia. "Are we forgiven?" She placed her hand over Mia's.

"Yes." Mia dropped her shoulders. "You did nothing wrong, Serena. I was angry Lily didn't contact me, but I understand why. I'm glad you're okay."

"We discussed it in more detail while we waited for you," Lily said. "All's good, and I'm forgiven."

"Lily, do you still think Teddy murdered Ava?" Serena asked.

"Yes, and no. But, you're innocent until proven guilty."

"That's how I feel," Serena said. "Besides, Sam doesn't think he did it."

"Sam?" Mia and Lily said in unison.

"You know. My fish. Have I told you about Samurai?"

"Maybe?" Mia wrinkled her nose. "It's nice you have a place to go when things get overwhelming. Grandmother swears she does her best thinking at the pond."

"The fish listen, Mia," Serena said. "Nina may have a telepathic bond with one. Knowing her, she has connections with them all."

"True." Mia nodded. "I never doubt anything that happens at The Pearl. Telepathic koi might be a thing."

"I want one," Lily said, sticking out her lower lip.

"I think they choose you." Serena cringed. "Sorry." She took one more sip of tea. "I need to get to the bar. See what's taking place there. Consider what I said about Teddy. Love you."

After a round of air kisses, Serena hurried to the front of the gardens. She heard a woman's voice shouting at someone by the exit. *Isabella?*

"There are no taxis? No rideshares available? This is a big city. What's going on?" Isabella berated the young man standing at the taxi and limo station.

"I'm sorry, but everyone is leaving at the same time," he said. "Our airport limo is scheduled to return in fifteen or twenty minutes."

"I have a plane to catch," Isabella hissed.

"Perhaps I can be of service," Serena said, stepping between the two. "I'm a rideshare driver. What apps do you have?"

Isabella sneered and held out her phone. "You drive people for a living? I thought you were an author."

"It's a reputable job, Isabella." Serena pointed to the app. "That one. I'll wait over there until you're finished." She strolled to the Torii gate, not believing her good fortune. *Isabella trapped in a car with me. I can ask questions, and she can't escape.*

Serena shot a glance toward the pond. *Did you intervene and make this possible, Sam?* She shook her head. *No way.*

"Well? Come on. If you can drive me to the airport, let's go." Isabella stood in front of Serena, hand on hip.

"I need to give the valet my number." Serena waited for the automatic doors to open and walked to the outdoor stand. She never checked to see if Isabella followed, but the sound of heels clicking against the pavement proved she was.

"What airline?" Serena asked, facing the woman.

"One that takes me home to Brazil," Isabella snarled. "Far from here."

"Tough weekend."

"Very."

"Who do you think did it?" Serena saw her car coming towards them and asked, "Front or back?"

"Back is fine."

The valet opened Isabella's door, then circled around to the driver's side. After Serena generously tipped him, she slid behind the wheel. When she checked the rearview mirror, Isabella had her compact open, applying lipstick. "So, as I was saying…" Serena continued.

"Who do I think did it?" Isabella asked. "It is not for me to say. Although I have heard it is the photographer. The little nervous man. Ava did not like him."

Serena drove away from the hotel and within minutes she'd reached the highway. "Ted told me few people liked Ava."

"That is not true!" Isabella exclaimed in a cross voice. "Ava and I were friends. Close friends."

She can say anything now. "Really? Did you have sleepovers and braid each other's hair?"

"You should not joke at a time like this, Serena. It sounds like you do not believe me. I can prove we were friends."

"Most of Ava's life is public information," Serena replied. "What do you know others don't?'

"Shoe size."

"Public info."

"No. Her proper shoe size. Ava was embarrassed by her huge feet. She always requested size nine when really, she was a ten."

"Okay, I didn't know, but someone might. Besides, lots of people wear size ten. What's the big deal? Maybe you have the answer to that?"

"Ooh! Why am I trying to prove anything to you?"

"Because I think you killed her."

"What? Pull over. I need to get out. Pull over this instant."

"I can't. We're on a highway."

Isabella pounded on the passenger front seat. "You are an evil woman, Serena. This is the reason you are taking me to the airport, isn't it? To get me to confess to something I did not do."

"Calm down," Serena said in a soothing, motherly tone. "I wanted to get a reaction."

"You believe me?" Isabella sniffed.

"Maybe. I hope you are innocent," Serena said, pulling up to Isabella's airline. "If you're not, I'm flying to Brazil to get you and drag you back to California by your hair."

"Ooh, I'm scared." Isabella hopped from the car. "Goodbye. And I hope your next book is an enormous flop."

"Thanks." Serena waved. She checked her app and saw Isabella did not leave a tip. "What did I expect? I accused her of murder."

Serena clung to the steering wheel, contemplating her next move. She tapped her fingers along the leather, considering her choices. "I think I'll pay a visit to the police station."

Chapter Twelve

"I'm here to see Ted Lewis." Serena showed her ID to an officer behind the plexiglass. "If there's a problem, please call Detective Jack Ando."

"Have a seat," the officer instructed.

Ten minutes later, a police officer escorted Serena through a corridor to a compact room containing a table and two chairs. Teddy sat in one, leaning forward with his elbows on the tabletop, head in hands.

"Teddy?"

Teddy glanced up, and Serena noticed red, swollen eyes. He needed a shave, and his clothes were wrinkled. "What are you doing here?" he growled.

"I came as a friend." Serena took the seat across from him.

"To ask why I tried to kill you? That's how the cops see it. Attempted murder and murder one."

"Did you try to kill me?

Teddy slowly shook his head. "No, I wanted to stop you from speaking with Detective Ando before I got the chance to leave. I hoped you'd sleep all morning. It would give me time to reach the airport and catch my flight."

"I told you I thought you were innocent."

"Doesn't matter. They think I did it. I booked a flight to Mexico yesterday, arranged for a car to pick me up at five a.m. this morning and went to the airport. I hoped to blend in before my flight."

"The police found you before you boarded?"

"Yes." Teddy threw out his hands. "And here I am."

"I'm sorry." Serena tapped the table. "What type of sleeping pill did you put in my drink?"

"Something my mom takes. Since my stay in rehab, I can't get a prescription. I borrow a few when I go on assignment." Teddy made air quotes when he said "borrow".

"Let's hope it doesn't match what someone gave Ava." Serena grimaced. "They took *my* blood for comparison."

"Still won't matter, Serena. They want to wrap this up quickly, and I look guilty as sin. I even tried to flee the country."

"Fear took over."

"Darn right, it did. The conversation we had the first day now becomes incriminating evidence. I was so relieved when you said you hadn't spoken to the detective yet. But then, I realized you'd eventually tell him, and I needed to get out of the hotel ASAP."

"We're waiting on the results of the bloodwork, but if it shows the drug differs from Ava's, I'll do what I can." Serena pushed her chair back, ready to leave.

"Wait. Before you go. Think. Am I allowed in the dressing room? No. Would Ava allow me to serve her a glass of champagne? No. Ask Jonathan if I was anywhere near the bar on Saturday. If given a chance, I can find witnesses who'd place me outside in the garden, setting up my equipment *all* morning."

"Okay, I'll talk to Jonathan and search for witnesses. I'll start with The Pearl staff." *And Lily.*

"Thank you, Serena," Teddy cried. "I'm sorry I was mean when you first arrived."

"It was nothing. Remember, I have two teenagers." Serena lifted one side of her mouth.

"Speaking of them, I got some fantastic shots. When I'm cleared, I'll send them to you."

"Hang in there, Teddy," Serena encouraged, knocking on the door to signal she was ready to exit.

* * * *

Serena sat in her car, staring at the police station. *I missed something but still have no clue.* Before starting the engine, she sent a text to Mia: *Quiz Lily on her whereabouts Saturday morning. Ask how often she saw Teddy and what he was doing. Will you question The Pearl staff members who worked the show and ask about him?*

Torn between home and the hotel, Serena steered the car towards home. *I need to give Mia time to question people. Besides, the girls need me.* Guilt rushed through her when she thought about the last two days. She hadn't been home and had only sent the occasional text. *Like Justice.*

She smirked. *The girls don't know Justice. Not really. They've barely seen him in six years. I assumed they'd be okay. I should have insisted he see them more often.* She pounded the steering wheel. "Justice! I don't want you back, so why are you still driving me crazy?"

Her mom's car sat in the driveway with another behind it. *Justice?* Serena had no idea what kind of car he drove during the cooler weather. Usually, he rode a motorcycle.

"I'm home," Serena called from the back entrance of her home.

It felt good to step into a warm, inviting atmosphere. She inhaled the familiar scent and noticed a new one. "Mom's baking or just finished."

Jewel and Jade ran through the kitchen and greeted her in the mudroom. "Mom, we've been so worried," Jewel said, throwing her arms around Serena's neck.

Jade rubbed her mom's back. "We're proud of you, Mom. You proved your innocence."

"I'm not done yet, girls. I returned home to check on you, then I must head back."

"It's okay," Jewel said. "You're doing the right thing."

Surprised by her comment, Serena replied, "I am?"

"Yes, you taught us to see things through to the end," Jade answered. "How could we be upset that you were gone? You didn't choose to stay. The police wouldn't let you leave. Also, you are the coolest mom. You got us a part in the fashion show. It turned into a murder investigation, but we got to walk. We'll never forget it. I love you."

"So do I," Jewel said. "May I also remind you we don't need babysitters? Haven't in years. Plus, we turn eighteen soon."

"Don't remind me." Serena rolled her eyes and teased, "Knowing you two, a party would start the minute I walked out the door." She laughed, wrapping her arms around the girls.

"Good to see you home," Justice said, entering the room.

"Thanks," Serena answered, letting go of the twins. "You can go now. I'm here." *Soon to leave again, but you don't know that.* "Where's Mama?"

"In the family room watching her show," Justice answered. "She invited me to stay for dinner."

"Did she now." Serena held down the anger she felt. "I need to speak with her."

"First, I'd like to talk with you," Justice said. "Girls, do you mind?"

"No, Daddy, not at all." Jade took Jewel's hand and walked out to the kitchen.

Daddy? "What?" Serena used the most annoyed voice she could muster.

"Hey, baby, I wanted to see if you are alright." Justice placed his hands on her shoulders. "Come here. I bet it's been tough, especially when they accused you of murder."

Instantly, Serena wanted to protect Jack. She bent her arms up and pushed Justice's hands from her shoulders. "The police suspect many people. They were doing their job."

"Right, and they decided *you* were guilty."

"Stop. I had the means and opportunity."

"Ooh, look at you, using cop language."

"I forgot motive. I had that, too." Serena pushed past him and headed into the kitchen.

"Serena, wait." Justice grasped her arm. "I'm sorry. I know this is serious."

Before she got the chance to pull away, Serena was in his arms. Justice kissed her with such passion it might have made her toes curl, but today she cringed and didn't return the kiss.

"What's wrong?" he asked.

"This." Serena gave him a punch to his gut.

"Hey? Why did you do that?" Justice gasped for a breath.

"You don't grab someone and kiss them without their permission."

"We were married," Justice protested.

"Not anymore. You are my ex-husband, Justice. Emphasis on ex."

Justice slid his hand into Serena's. "We could change that. Get married again. Remember the good times we had? We'd fill a picnic basket and ride up to the mountains. Find a secluded place and…" He wiggled his eyebrows. "Let's go for a ride this weekend."

"It's the end of February," Serena replied with a shudder.

"Then we go in my car." Justice squeezed her hand. "Think about it."

"I did. The answer is no." Serena tugged her hand from his grip. "I think you should go."

"What about dinner?"

"I'll eat your portion." Serena folded her arms over her chest.

"Okay, fine." Justice held his hands up in surrender. "Before I go, may I say you're as beautiful as any model and have a much better body. Not all skin and bones."

"Thanks for the compliment…I think." Serena nudged him toward the back entrance. "I appreciated you helping while I was away."

Justice paused at the door. "Think about this weekend."

"I thought we covered the subject."

"If not the mountains, I'll take you anywhere. We'll call it our official first date."

"We won't."

"Tell the girls I said goodbye."

"I certainly will." Serena breathed a sigh of relief when the door closed. "Does that man have trouble hearing?" She shook her head. "Or only hears what he chooses to hear."

Past events shuffled through her mind like a movie trailer. When it came time to meet her parents, Justice had arrived an hour late to the restaurant. He'd heard the name of the place but not much else. Serena had brushed it off, but her father, rest his soul, had given her a speech about what to expect in the future. On the day of their wedding, Justice had shown up to the church late and noticeably drunk. "You told me to celebrate with my boys," he'd said. "A champagne toast, right?" "One glass," Serena had replied. "Not eight bottles."

Over the years, Serena learned Justice had selective hearing. The same applied when it came to their girls. Justice heard dinner and assumed he could eat any time. He missed baths and bedtimes, thinking he did nothing wrong. Serena grew tired of reminding him of daily chores and paying bills. She ended up doing most household tasks herself.

Serena blew through her lips. "I needed to relive those moments. Remind myself of how it was. The way Justice perceives our married life differs from mine."

"Hello, sweetie." Her sixty-five-year-old mother stood in the doorway. Serena favored her in many ways. She was blessed with her perfect skin and both their brown eyes had flecks of gold. Her mom pushed her oversized glasses up her nose, which was like Serena's.

"Mama, I was coming to see you."

"It's okay, darling, I need to start dinner."

"Let me treat. Takeout, delivery, go to a restaurant. You choose."

"Absolutely not," her mother answered. "You sit and put your feet up while I get things going. We need to talk."

Oh, no. "Sure, about what?"

"You've worked two jobs for so long, sweetheart. I applaud you for how you handled the last six years. I am always happy to help when needed."

"Where is this conversation going, Mama?"

"What if I move in for the next few months? I promise it won't be long term. I'll leave when the girls go off to college."

"You'd do that?" Serena asked.

"This year your life changed overnight." Her mom counted on her fingers. "Published author. Book signings. Flying to events. You don't keep regular hours anymore. You need someone at the house."

Serena rushed to her mom and embraced her tightly. "Thank you," she whispered.

"You can let go now." Her mom chuckled.

"What made you decide to move in now?" Serena cocked her head.

"I'd come anytime. All you had to do was ask. But you didn't."

"You have your own life, Mama. Card group, church, choir…"

"Hush. I'll still do those things."

"Then, yes, please move in until the girls leave for college."

"You may not want me to move back home once I'm here." Her mom winked.

"True. I'd have a live-in cook," Serena teased.

"And baker." Her mom touched Serena's arm. "You need time to work on your next book. Running a home, watching over two rambunctious teens and working takes a lot out of you." Her mom closed one eye. "You have started the next book, haven't you?"

"Um, yeah, I'm working on it."

"Sounds like a no. More reason for me to be here." Her mom popped a casserole into the oven. "I'll let that bake for forty-five minutes. It's your favorite. Chicken, broccoli, rice."

"And cheese?"

"Oh, yes, darling, there's cheese."

"I needed some comfort food tonight, Mama, but you were the biggest comfort of all."

* * * *

After dinner, Serena's phone pinged. *Mia.* Her message read: *Are you coming back tonight? Should we call a P.I.C. meeting? I have information.*"

Yes, to all, Serena typed back. She looked at her family sitting around the kitchen table. Before she said a word, her mom said, "Go. We've got this."

Her mom rose from her chair and escorted Serena to the back door. "You're an inspiration to your girls, Serena. I'm proud of you."

Tears welled in Serena's eyes. "I try my best."

"It's all anyone can ask. Now go help solve that crime and get some ideas for your book."

"You knew?" Serena wrinkled her nose.

"Yes, you need outside stimulation. The way you see the world, and your ability to notice the finer details in life, set you apart from most people. You're tuned into the subtle nuances that often elude the rest of us. This quality helps you turn real events into compelling novels. Do you agree?" Serena's mother smiled warmly. Her sunny expression always had the power to lift Serena's spirits.

"Wow." Serena kissed her mom on the cheek. "You get me. You really get me."

Chapter Thirteen

"Serena, you've been gone a long time," Jack said, catching up to her after she entered the hotel.

"Sorry, did you need me?" Serena stopped in front of the office hallway, and their eyes connected, causing her heart to skip a beat.

"Not really." Jack stepped closer. "I thought you said you were coming back sooner."

"I got distracted, then guilt took over. I went home to check on the girls." Serena hoped he'd accept her answer. She didn't want to mention Justice, the kiss or the marriage proposal. "Any suspects in the bar?"

"No, but I told them to stay in the hotel. If they leave, we'll know." Jack pressed his lips together. "Besides, the hotel needed to open the bar. Guests weren't too happy that it was closed. While the rooftop one has ambiance, it doesn't appeal to some people in cooler weather. The hotel has placed outdoor propane torches to warm the area, yet certain guests prefer indoors. Speaking of bars, how about a drink later? We can compare notes."

"Sounds great," Serena did an internal happy dance.

"I hoped you stayed out of trouble today," Jack teased.

"Oh, I did," Serena lied. "What time should we meet?"

"I need to go to the station. I haven't heard from Sue yet. Your test results must be done by now. I'll grab some takeout, eat there and be back by eight. I can text you if I'm running late."

"How?" Serena held up her phone. "Do you have my number?"

"Um, yes." Jack took her cell. "Do you mind?" Serena nodded and watched him enter his number into her phone. "So you'll know it's me," he said, returning the phone. "I won't keep you. I spotted you as I was about to leave."

"I planned to stop by my office," Serena winced. *A small lie. Jack can't know about Partners in Crime. He'd put a stop to it.*

"See you later?" Jack saluted and went toward the exit.

Serena checked the blouse and jeans she was still wearing from this morning. *It has been a long day. I can't wear this. Hopefully, the girls packed something nice when they brought me clothes.* Changing her direction, Serena passed through the Torii gate and followed the path to the tearoom. When she arrived, Mia stood at the entrance.

Excitement over her date with Jack had built up during the walk, and when she saw her friend, she exclaimed, "Jack asked me out."

"Really?"

"Probably not." Serena hung her head. "He wants to compare notes."

"Tell me exactly what he said." Mia guided Serena to their table. "I'll be the judge."

"Something like, 'How about a drink later?' Does it sound like a date?" Serena lifted her shoulder.

"Maybe. Jack keeps his emotions in check. He's hard to read. I'm leaning toward a date."

"I hope I have something to wear." Serena waved her hand along her wrinkled blouse. "The girls must have packed a dress."

"Don't worry," Mia said. "I've got you covered. What size are you?"

"I fit into your plus-size category," Serena answered. "Twelve."

"Stop. It's not plus-size. Only in the fashion world." Mia rolled her eyes. "I have the perfect dress. Shoe size?"

"Eight."

"Mind if I come to your room and help you dress?" Mia lifted her brows.

"Really?" Mia appeared happy for her.

"Yes. Jack won't know what hit him." Mia nodded toward the entrance. "Lily is here. I passed along your message about Teddy."

"Hey." Lily sat down with a huff. "Quite the day, right?" She turned to Serena. "I heard you drove Isabella to the airport. How did it go?"

"Not well. I accused her of murdering Ava, and she responded with claims of their strong friendship. I asked for proof."

Lily nodded. "She can say whatever she wants now."

"That's what I said." Serena tipped her cup in Lily's direction.

"What proof did she give?" Mia asked.

"Ava's shoe size." Serena smirked. "Anyone can look it up."

"What size did she say?" Mia scrolled on her phone. "I have the model's details here."

"Size nine."

"That's what I have. Isabella didn't prove a thing."

"There's more to the story. Isabella claims only she knew the truth. Ava wore a size ten."

"News to me." Mia shrugged. "But I'm not the dresser. I'll text Enrique."

While Mia typed, Serena prepared her tea. "I'm glad this tearoom is open for breakfast, lunch and dinner. Most aren't. It's usually a lunch thing."

"Originally, it was only open for lunch," Lily answered. "It got so popular that Nina changed the hours. Beneficial for us. It's an excellent place to meet."

Serena perused the menu. "I already ate dinner, but the choices are tempting."

"Agree." Lily smiled.

"Lily," Serena said. "Can you recall the events from Saturday? Was Teddy missing for an extended period?"

"I didn't watch him every minute," Lily responded. "He was in and out of the reception hall, checking lighting and finding the perfect spot to set up his equipment."

"How did he act?"

"I only met him this weekend, but I didn't see any changes in his behavior."

"There." Mia held up her phone. "I got an answer."

Enrique's text message said: *Size 9.*

"Okay." Serena let out a breath. "I'll let it go for now. We need to clear Teddy before going after the actual killer."

Mia had ordered a plate of Serena's favorite almond cookies. When the server arrived, she placed a three-tiered tray in the center of the table filled with the mouth-watering treats. Serena savored the rich taste as she bit into one. A sip of oolong, and she was a new woman.

"What about you, Mia?" Serena asked. "Did you talk to the hotel staff?"

"I spoke to people assigned to work in the garden and ballroom. Most remember Teddy. They said he was polite and asked permission to move things. He stayed out of their way, and no one noticed him leaving for an extended time. Not one person thought he acted strangely or in an unusual way."

"Oh! One more thing," Serena said. "I went to the police station to visit Teddy."

"You didn't," Lily answered in a low, dramatic voice.

"I needed to see him. Look him in the eye."

"What did you discover?" Mia asked.

"A sad man who feels cornered," Serena answered. "I'm still not sure if he's guilty. Hopefully, Jack has the drug test results when I meet him tonight."

"Did I miss something?" Lily widened her eyes.

Mia leaned forward. "Serena has a date with Jack."

"It's not a date-date. We're meeting to discuss the case." Serena bit her lip, fighting back a smile.

"You go, girl," Lily said.

"Speaking of going," Mia replied. "Serena, go upstairs, and I'll visit the dressing room to choose some dresses."

"Can I come?" Lily rubbed her hands together.

"Yes," Serena answered. "Please join Mia and make sure she picks something I'd wear on a first date." She rolled her eyes. "And not too revealing."

* * * *

Serena barely had time to fix her hair before the knock came. She'd left the ballerina bun in place and worked on smoothing her hair and refreshing her makeup. "Coming."

Lily and Mia looked like two excited teens who'd shopped at a high-end boutique. "Please try them on," Lily begged. "My vote goes to…"

"Don't influence her, Lily." Mia handed her three bags and one box of shoes. "The shoes should go with each dress."

Serena hurried into the bedroom and unzipped the first bag. A one-shoulder, single long sleeve black mini dress appeared. Inside the box, she found neutral color, pointed-toed shoes with a black patent leather shaped heart on each toe. When she touched the dress, it felt soft and buttery. "Is this real leather?"

After dressing, Serena examined the look in the full-length mirror. "Too sexy? I do like it." She opened the bedroom door and heard Lily gasp. "Well?" she asked.

"It's my fav," Lily said.

"Lily, you don't get to vote unless Serena asks," Mia reminded her. "Two more to go, Serena."

Moving on to the second dress, Serena discovered a deep rose sleeveless mini dress with a fun fringe around the bottom. She studied herself in the mirror, checking front and back. The fringe moved with her.

After modeling the second dress, Serena continued on to the last dress. She caught a peek of the jade green color and instantly fell in love. Pulling the sleeveless mini dress from its bag, she examined the black lines running through it in a large diamond pattern. She slipped it on and checked in the mirror. The dress had a mock turtleneck in solid jade green and hugged her body in the right places.

"This is the one," she cried, walking out to the sitting area. "I love it."

"I'm glad you love it. Keep it," Mia said. "And the others."

"No, it's too much."

"After what I put you through, I insist."

"You did nothing, Mia," Serena said.

"How can you say that? It's my fault the police accused you of murder." Mia sobbed into her hands.

"Oh, sweetie, it never crossed my mind." Serena rushed to the sofa and sat next to her. "I've been so busy clearing my name and finding the killer, I never thought how this affected you. *I* should apologize."

"No." Mia shook her head.

"I've had my head buried in tech," Lily said. "I never asked either of you if you needed to talk or cry on my shoulder."

"Let's do it now," Serena replied, and they wrapped and overlapped their arms around each other.

After the last sob, Lily said, "I'll get some tissues. Serena, you need to check your makeup."

The lighthearted statement made Serena giggle. She nudged Mia, who joined in. "Thanks again for the dress," Serena whispered.

* * * *

I'm at the bar, Jack texted.

Be down in a minute, Serena answered. "This is it," she said with a shiver of excitement.

"I'd love to see Jack's face when you walk in," Lily replied. "Have fun."

"Why am I so nervous?" Serena asked.

"You like him," Mia replied. "Just be yourself."

"Okay, here I go." Serena inhaled and opened the door. She let out the breath she held as she walked to the elevator. "Good evening, Jack." She practiced different voices on the way down to the lobby.

Stepping from the elevator, Serena noticed subtle glances and held her head high. *Perhaps they think I'm one of the models.* She pretended she was until she spotted Jack hopping up from a table, heading her way. Dressed in a tight black t-shirt and black jeans, Serena swallowed a few times, then smiled. "Good evening, Jack."

"You look amazing," Jack said, escorting her to the table. "Drink?"

"Gin and tonic," Serena answered, taking a seat.

"I'll be right back."

When Jack returned from ordering the drinks, he pulled his chair closer to Serena. He wore a shorter sleeved shirt than his uniform, and Serena noticed a partial tattoo peeking below the material. She touched his arm and said, "May I see it?"

He responded with a simple "Sure" and rolled up his sleeve. "It's calligraphy," Jack announced.

"What does it say?"

"Ryu, pronounced ree-yooh. It means dragon." Jack stared at her. "I know what you're thinking. Why didn't he get a dragon?"

"Not really, but please tell."

"I wanted the real thing, but my fiancée talked me into the symbols."

"You were married."

"Yes, for a short time."

"Did your wife get a matching tattoo?"

"No, she had a fear of needles."

Jonathan arrived at the table and served their drinks. "Gin and tonic for the lady. A beer for the gentleman."

"Jonathan, you're working. Do you ever get a break?" Serena asked.

"I might as well work. I can't leave the hotel." Jonathan flashed a death stare at Jack.

Jack held his gaze. "I'm sorry, Jonathan. It's not personal."

"Drinks on me," Jonathan replied and strode back to the bar.

"He's angry," Serena said. "You don't have enough evidence to clear him?"

"Not yet," Jack answered. "Hey, I know I said we should meet to discuss the case, but I'd rather hear about your day."

The change in topic came as a pleasant surprise. *Maybe this is a date.* Serena shared her rideshare experience, leaving out no detail. To her delight, Jack burst into laughter as she vividly described Isabella pounding on the back of the passenger seat, swearing in Spanish. She enjoyed the sound and wished she could hear him laugh more often. Jack then became serious when she discussed Teddy but appeared to know she'd gone to the station.

"Now I want to ask the million-dollar question," Serena said. "Did you get the results of my bloodwork?"

Chapter Fourteen

"I have your test results here." Jack opened his phone. "Ted Lewis used a milder sleeping pill compared to the one given to Ava."

Serena slapped the table. "I knew it."

Jack held up his hand. "I'm not done. He put more in your drink than the suggested dose."

"How bad?" Serena asked. "Enough to kill me?"

"No," Jack answered. "He hoped you'd sleep for a long time."

"That's what he told me, Jack. He wanted to escape before I talked to you. Please, investigate this," Serena pleaded. "He looks guilty as heck, but something tells me he didn't do it."

"*I* will do some more investigating, but you stay out of it." Jack set his beer on the table. "No more lady detective for you, even if it's for your book."

"You think I'm doing this for my next book?" Serena sat up taller. "Then you don't know me."

"I'd like to get to know you, Serena."

Jack's words prevented Serena from lecturing him. After all the drama, she had almost forgotten about her book.

"Speechless, for once?" Jack teased, although he appeared nervous.

"No, surprised. I can't read you," Serena answered. "You act professional, which comes with the job, but you never reveal your true self, your personality."

Jack swiped his hand from under his chin to the top of his pants. "This is me."

"The bad boy look?" Serena grinned. *Did I say bad boy? I had one and look how that turned out. No, don't judge him. Enjoy the night and see where this goes.*

"Is that what you'd call it?" Jack chuckled. "Let's say I'm not very good at fashion."

Serena held up her gin and tonic in a salute. "Join the club. Mia dressed me for tonight."

"You look fabulous, Serena." Jack touched his beer bottle to her glass.

Shivers permeated her body, and Serena caught a glimpse of the real man. She'd been so busy comparing him to Justice, she never took notice of his qualities. Some were quite the opposite of her ex. "I'll tell Mia you approve."

"You'll do no such thing. I'm complimenting you."

"Okay, you win."

"Thanks." Jack gave her a genuine smile. "Tell me more about your day. You took Isabella to the airport, then drove to the station to see Ted. What happened after that? Why didn't you come back here?"

"Mother's guilt took over, and I drove home. I needed to see the girls."

"Jade and Jewel, right?"

"Yes. Twins."

"Really? They don't look like each other." Jack paused. "They're fraternal twins. Jewel reminds me of you. She's quite the beauty."

"That's kind of you to say. I'll accept the compliment for her."

"Jade is, too. Only she doesn't look like her sister or you."

"Yep, you figured it out," Serena said. "She takes after her dad in more ways than one."

"Is she the rebel?" Jack chuckled.

"Yes, in a good way, not like…" Serena wrapped her hands around her drink. "I shouldn't talk about Justice."

"Was he with the girls when you got home?"

"My mom is staying at the house, but yes, he was there." Serena played with the straw, pushing the lime into the liquid. "He was on his way out. We barely talked."

"One day, I hope you'll share more," Jack said. "What about your mom?"

"Robin Baker, in case you want to run a background check." Serena teased.

"I didn't mean her name, Serena." The corner of Jack's mouth twitched. "She sounds like a fantastic mom."

"She is. I don't give her enough credit. Mama suggested moving in until the girls head off to college. Although my dad is no longer with us, she continues to live her own life. I wouldn't want her to abandon it. However, this arrangement would allow me time to work on my book."

"Since this weekend, I assume you've done no writing."

"Just notes. I've got lots of them."

"It's a start. How do you do it, Serena? Where do you start? I don't think I could write more than a chapter."

"Once you begin, it comes to you. If you have notes, you refer to them. Some authors make outlines before they start."

"You're the notebook type," Jack said.

Thrilled he wanted to know her family and how she wrote, Serena decided she should discover more about him. "What about your family, Jack?"

"My mom and dad live in L.A. I'm originally from there. I have a younger brother who works in sales. Dan travels all over California."

"Maybe I'll meet him one day."

"Maybe you will."

Serena nudged him. "I've got an idea, Jack. What if I sit at the bar and order two more drinks? While I wait, I'll interview Jonathan."

"What did I just tell you?" Jack ran his hand through his hair. He dropped his head and glanced at her from the corner of his eye. "You're determined, and I can't stop you. Am I correct?"

"See, you *are* getting to know me." Serena rose from her chair and tugged on her dress. "Here I go."

Walking toward the bar, Serena realized Jack could see her every move. *Take it slow. Walk like a model. The girls taught me well.* Not used to wearing three-inch spike heels daily, her ankle turned, causing her to stumble. Luckily, a bar stool saved her from falling. She looked over her shoulder and waved at Jack. *Ooh, he's trying not to laugh.*

Jonathan slid a towel along the bar and ended up in front of Serena. "What can I do for you?"

"Same as last time."

"One gin and tonic, one beer coming right up." Jonathan pointed at Serena. "Are you and the detective a thing?"

"We are not a thing." Serena made air quotes with her fingers. "Jack asked me to meet for drinks. It's not serious."

"The way you're dressed says serious." Jonathan wiggled his brows.

"Stop. Let's not talk about me anymore. We need to discuss your situation." Serena placed her hand on the bar. "You said you can't leave the hotel. You're still on the suspect list?"

"Yeah, along with two or three others," Jonathan answered. "You're so into this, I have a feeling you like crime shows."

"British ones, yes."

"Hey, me, too."

"You're kidding, right? Trying to get on my good side." Serena tilted her head.

"No, really, I enjoy watching them. The actors seem like real people."

"That's true. I like submerging myself into their world."

I like to play means, motive and opportunity while I watch." Johnathan blew through his lips. "When it comes to this crime, I fit under all the categories. I can't blame the detective for suspecting me."

"Let's play your game," Serena said. She questioned if Jonathan's willingness to share was to prove his innocence or divert attention from his possible guilt. "Start with means. Did you have the ability and tools to carry out the crime?"

"Look at me." Jonathan held out his hands. "I have the ability." He leaned on the bar and spoke softly. "Anyone can get their hands on drugs and easily slip it into a drink."

Serena's heart raced. *Is he threatening me? He's about to make my drink. No, he's smiling. Smiling? An evil grin, perhaps.* "Okay, you had the means. Maybe we should stop playing. Jack's waiting for his drink."

"Sure. I forgot you were on a date. Come back when we can continue." Jonathan winked.

Serena watched his every move as Jonathan prepared her gin and tonic. He popped off the beer bottle's cap, and she made sure his hand didn't slide over the opening. She struck a casual pose while she waited and thanked him when he delivered the beverages.

Her mind raced as she returned to the table. "Oh, my gosh, Jack," Serena said, setting down the drinks. "I've seen another side of Jonathan tonight. I thought he was a good guy but underneath he's crafty and manipulative."

"Whoa. Hold on there. During your brief conversation, you changed your mind about him?"

"It was his eyes." Serena held up two fingers and waved them in front of hers.

"I believe your passion for clearing Ted Lewis' name is clouding your judgement. I thought you liked Jonathan."

Serena dropped her shoulders and sighed. "I like him."

"If you want to become a true detective, you need to learn to be objective," Jack stated.

"So, we can start working together?" The thought brightened Serena's mood.

"I didn't say that." Jack slowly shook his head. "You are something."

"Thanks…if you meant it in a good way." Serena smiled.

Jack stroked her cheek with the back of his forefinger. "I do."

Serena closed her eyes and leaned in, anticipating their first kiss. Upon opening her eyes, she found Jack standing beside her, searching for his wallet. He threw a ten-dollar bill on the table. "Got to start early tomorrow. I'd like to bring this case to its conclusion quickly or is that too much to ask?" He chuckled. "May I walk you to the elevator?"

"No thanks. I think I'll stay for a while." Serena tried to keep the disappointment from her voice. "Are you going to the station tomorrow?"

"Yes, Sue and I are going over test results."

Sue. Serena pictured the petite brunette who she hadn't considered as competition, yet now she did. Sue was in the right age range, and Serena didn't notice a wedding band. "Tell her I said hi." *Why did I say that?*

"O…kay." Jack paused. "Anything else before I go?"

"Um, no. I'm good." Serena held back the questions she suddenly longed to ask. *How old is Sue? Is she married with kids? How well do you know her? Why am I acting like a jealous girlfriend? What the heck?* She stood and placed herself in front of Jack. *What do I have to lose?*

Serena tenderly rested her lips on Jack's. "Goodnight," she said, and strutted to the bar.

* * * *

"Let me do motive," Serena said, sipping the iced tea she'd ordered. "You were attracted to Ava, and she rejected you. A reason to commit the crime."

"If your statement was true, we'd be murdering each other quite often." Jonathan laughed.

"This is different. Ava Taylor was a supermodel. She toyed with you. Ava flirted to get what she wanted. Did that make you angry?"

"Not angry but hurt. My job was beneath her. She made it abundantly clear that she couldn't be seen with a bartender. I didn't stand a chance. Then, when she wanted something, she'd sidle up next to me, kiss my cheek and wrap her arm around my waist."

"And you did her bidding."

"I must do as she asked, Serena. I work here."

"True, but I meant the extra perks. Going the extra mile without being asked."

"Again, I work here." Jonathan turned over his hand. "Please the customer. That's The Pearl's motto."

"You make an excellent argument," Serena said. "But opportunity stands out the most. You delivered the champagne to Ava and had time to slip drugs into her drink or the bottle."

"Never the bottle." Jonathan pointed at Serena. "You never know who else may take a drink. The person must put in the glass."

Surprised by his revelation, Serena wondered if he was confessing or using another tactic to distract her. "You slipped the drug into her drink?"

"I meant in general," Jonathan answered. "Not me."

"Do you pour her first glass?"

"Usually."

"What about the day of the show?"

"Excuse me, bartender, can I order a drink?" a man's voice called from the other end of the bar.

"Sorry, Serena, I must take care of these people. Bar gets busy this time of night."

"Go ahead. I'll sit here and finish my tea." Serena mulled over what she'd learned. Jonathan had the means, motive and opportunity to commit the crime. *Especially opportunity. He delivered the champagne to the dressing room.*

Something about that bothered her. *What is it?* Her brain went into action, sorting out the activities of her day. Part of a conversation she'd had with Teddy came to mind. She was about to leave when Teddy called to her. *Wait. Before you go. Think. Am I allowed in the dressing room? No. Would Ava allow me to serve her a glass of champagne? No. Ask Jonathan if I was anywhere near the bar on Saturday.*

Serena toyed with her phone, wishing she had her notebook. *I didn't ask Jonathan if Teddy was here Saturday morning. I can wait a few more minutes.* When she noticed a lull at the bar, Serena motioned to Jonathan.

"I see you're still here. What's up?" he asked.

"I need to ask you a few questions before I go to my room," Serena replied.

"Sure." Jonathan wiped at a nonexistent spot on the bar.

"Did Ted Lewis ever come into the bar on Saturday morning?"

"Yes, he did."

"Taking photos perhaps?"

"No, he sat at the bar and ordered a bottle of champagne and one glass."

Chapter Fifteen

When Serena woke the next morning, she dashed off a text to Jack. She asked if the forensic lab had finished checking the champagne bottles and if glasses were included.

Jack promptly answered back, saying he'd arrived at the station and would get back to her when he had the information. Serena danced around the room. "He'll get back to me." She stopped spinning and bounced onto the mattress, hugging her phone to her chest.

Her happiness was short-lived as the last conversation of the evening interrupted her thoughts. Teddy had lied to her. He'd gone to the bar on Saturday morning. She didn't have the heart to go to the station and confront him. Instead, she chose to go to her office and begin working on her book. She'd thought of a more fitting title and needed to get the words on paper. *Mia and Lily will like it.*

A shower helped lift her spirits. "I can't let this case consume me. I have a life. Speaking of my personal life, I'll give Mama a call after I finish." Finding a peach shirt in her luggage, Serena paired it with a sea green skirt. A pair of black pumps finished the outfit. *A professional look may help me with the writing process.* Serena moved to the sitting area, hitting her mom's number as she walked.

"Hello, Serena," Robin said. "We're good here. You don't need to worry."

"I trust you have things under control, Mama. I called to see if the girls got off to school okay. And to thank you again."

"The girls are angels, Serena. I only give them one reminder to complete their chores or join me for dinner. I'd also fix them a big breakfast, but all they want is those bars. Is that food?"

"To them it is." Serena chuckled. Although she longed to inquire how Robin got the girls to listen, she decided not to ask. "I had a date last night."

"What? You haven't gone out in years. Good for you."

"He's handsome and charming, Mama. Kind and thoughtful."

"That's quite a reference, sweetie. If he makes you happy, I'll love him to bits."

"It's not serious. Don't start planning a wedding."

"Can I say a little prayer?"

"I'd appreciate it." Serena smiled. "I'm going to start my book today, right after breakfast."

"Wonderful news," Robin said.

"Have a good day, Mama."

"You, too, my darling." Robin paused. "You are in such a wonderful mood. I don't want to ruin it."

Serena dropped her shoulders. "You just did. What is it?"

"Before the girls left, they announced Justice would pick them up after school. I was about to call you when my phone rang, and it was you. Is that alright? Does he have permission?"

"We share custody, so he does, but I don't like it. He's never done it before." Serena's thoughts turned to her next course of action. *Call Justice.* "Mama, I'm going to take care of this. You are not to worry. Okay?"

"I'll try." Robin let out a breath. "I always liked Justice…to a point. The man is charismatic, but it doesn't make him a good husband or father. He won't do anything deceitful when he picks up the girls, will he?"

"Like kidnap them? No. But after years of radio silence, I want to know why he's suddenly father of the year."

"I agree. I spent some time with him before you came home yesterday. He regrets not spending time with the girls. Justice even mentioned he'd like to remarry you. But I read between the lines."

"That's my mama."

"I'm on your side, darling. The Baker girls stick together."

"Since we do, give me your opinion of why Justice is suddenly showing interest in our lives. I want to see if it matches mine."

"Your book, for one. He'd love to know how much money you've made."

"Does he now? Hmm. Tell him the author always gets paid last," Serena said. "Publishers, agents, and the printers come first. That's why authors want to sell a million copies."

"And you have, but I won't share that," Robin stated. "He never spent enough time with the girls, either. Before this weekend, Justice hadn't noticed the beautiful women they've become. He saw them as his little girls. The fashion show opened his eyes."

"Sorry you couldn't see them walk in the show," Serena said. "The show sold out."

"I didn't expect to come, Serena. This was Mia's first event at The Pearl. She's been so kind, giving me perks at the hotel. My friends think I'm royalty there."

"Tearoom, right?"

"Yes, I had book club there once, and they couldn't stop talking about it. The girls want to go back, but I am reluctant. I don't want to take advantage of Mia's kindness. Last time, she wouldn't let me pay a dime."

"That's my Mia," Serena replied. "Now, back to the twins. Do you think Justice wants to use them?"

"Yes, and no. He sees their potential as smart human beings and is a proud parent. But at the hotel, Justice learned about your connection to the Takeda family. If Mia helps you and the girls…?"

"Why not him," Mia whispered. "He wants to marry me for the wrong reasons."

"What did you say? Justice asked you to marry him?" Robin sounded so surprised Serena pictured her mom placing her hand over her heart.

"Yes, when I came home yesterday."

"He wasted no time. When he said he'd like to remarry you, I thought he meant someday."

"He's a fast worker." Serena's phone signaled she had another call. She glanced at the screen, and it showed Jack's name. "Mama, I've got another call. I'll speak with you later. Don't worry. This will all work out." She switched to the other call and said, "Jack?"

"Serena, I got the information you wanted. All the champagne bottles tested negative for drugs. Only one glass was positive." He paused. "Serena, are you there? I was ready for a barrage of questions."

"Yes, Jack, I am." Serena took a minute to get her bearings. "Would that evidence point more to Jonathan than Teddy?"

"We're leaning that way."

"You and Sue?"

"No, Bill and I. Hey, are you okay?"

It all came pouring out in one long breath. Serena held back tears, but when she finished, they trailed down her cheeks.

"Justice wants to remarry you?" Jack asked.

"Is that all you got from my sad tale?"

"No, sorry. What about this? You and I go to the high school when it lets out and speak with Justice."

"It's kind of you to offer, Jack. I plan to call him after we hang up. It could be a misunderstanding."

"Offer stands," Jack said. "I'll be here most of the day. Text or call, okay?"

"I will." Serena ended the call, laid back on the bed and stared at the ceiling. "What's a girl to do?" She rolled to her side and hit Justice's number. "Call her ex and unravel the mystery."

"Hey, Serena, glad you called," Justice said.

"What are you up to?" Serena growled.

"Is that how you greet the man who proposed to you?"

"If I remember correctly, you didn't get down on one knee with a ring and pop the question."

"I can if you wish. Change your mind about our date?"

"No, I'm calling about the girls."

"A dad can't treat them to burgers and shakes after a hard day at school?"

"Is that the plan?"

"Yeah, I intend to take them to that drive-in burger spot where you can order from your car, and they deliver a tray of food for you to enjoy."

"They've done it before." Serena thought of all the dinners they had there after a long day at work. *I didn't want to cook, and the twins always ordered the same meal.*

"The girls seemed excited." Justice's voice brought Serena back to the present.

"Okay, fine," Serena answered. "Have them home in two hours. If you don't, I'll call the police."

"Whoa. Slow down. No need to bring in the police. It's an innocent outing with my daughters."

"Which you've never done before. Also, I asked you a question and haven't gotten an answer yet. What are you up to?"

"Do you think I have ulterior motives, Serena?"

"Look, Justice, besides holidays and birthdays, we haven't heard from you until I wrote the book, and the girls walked in a fashion show. It piqued your interest. Suddenly, we're not just ex-wife and daughters anymore." Serena sat up, ready to do battle. "Before you say one word, I'll do the talking. It took hard work and determination to get to this point in our lives. You weren't part of our journey during the teen years. The difficult years. It's like the story of *The Little Red Hen*. I'm the hen and you're the duck, cat or dog or all three of them rolled into one."

"What?"

"You don't remember reading the book to the girls? Oh, right, I did. The hen wanted to bake bread and asked the animals to help gather ingredients. They refused. Who ate the bread when it came out of the oven? The hen and her children. When the animals begged for some, they got nothing. The red hen enjoyed the product of her hard work." *Get the analogy? Probably not.*

"Ooh, that's dirty, Serena, comparing me to a children's book."

"Did I get my point across?"

"Yes, and I'm trying to make it up to you and the girls. Will you let me?"

Serena sighed. "To the girls. Only them."

"See you tonight?"

"I'll be at the house. Remember the time limit."

"Two hours. Got it."

Serena ended the call before he tried to get on her good side even more. She texted the girls, *Dad is to bring you home after two hours*, and sent off a similar one to her mom.

* * * *

The concept she envisioned for her novel had crumbled by the time Serena reached her office. She ended up pacing the floor, debating if she'd done the right thing. Her daughters were her priority, but in another month, the twins would become adults. They had freedom of choice. She couldn't stop them from going to their dad's home or having dinner dates or shopping with him.

Serena returned to her swivel chair and stared at the title she'd typed. "*High Heels and High Stakes*. I think it works. My model will have a passionate love affair with a photographer and drop him before the most prestigious show of the season. He's so devastated he takes horrible pictures and loses his job. Of course, everyone suspects him of murder, but did he do it?"

Two hours passed, and Serena stared at her computer screen as thoughts ran through her mind. The page was still blank. She had written nothing. "The photographer needs an alibi. A good one," she told the screen. "I can't start this until we catch Ava's killer. What if Teddy did it?"

Serena glanced at the clock, panicking over the time. *Four-thirty*. She wanted to be home by five, ahead of Justice and the girls. Grabbing her cell, she requested her car from the valet station and texted Jack that she'd see him tomorrow.

"I've wasted an entire day. I didn't write or work on the case." Serena shook her head. "But tomorrow is a new day. First thing, I'm heading to the police station to speak with Teddy."

When Serena pulled into her driveway and opened the garage door, she discovered her mom had parked in one of the spaces. "She always left her car in the drive. Good for her. She feels at home."

Robin greeted her at the entry door. "You made it in time."

"Yep, and Justice had better come on time, too," Serena declared, settling onto the mudroom's bench to remove her shoes. "Much better. I've worn these all day."

"You look quite professional, darling," Robin said. "Did you get any writing done?"

"What do you think?" Serena grimaced.

"You felt overwhelmed, Serena. I'm worried, too."

"Mama." Serena stood and took Robin by her shoulders. "We can't do this anymore. I accomplished one thing today and faced the fact my twins are adults. We need to let them fly but know we're here for them. We're a safe place to land."

"I hope I did the same for you." Robin pulled Serena into her arms and hugged her tightly. "You're still my little girl."

"Ma. Enough." Serena giggled, then tilted her head. "I think I hear a car. Let's move to the other room."

Jade and Jewel entered the kitchen without saying a word. Serena checked their expressions, searching for any signs of trauma.

"Did you have fun?" Robin asked.

"It was okay," Jade answered.

"Just okay?"

"You know how Dad is, Grandma," Jewel said. "Hot and cold. We don't expect this to become a reoccurring event. Besides." She brought her index finger to her chin. "He asked a lot of questions about Mom and Mia."

Serena kept her anger in check. "Like what?" she asked.

"Dumb stuff," Jade replied. "We didn't give him too much information."

Serena was ready to burst. "Like?"

"I told him you met Mia when she was your rideshare passenger. Dad laughed at that. He said, 'Leave it to Serena to pick up a rich customer and become friends with her.' We defended you. You had no idea who she was."

"Anything else?"

"Tell her," Jewel said.

"I slipped up, Mom. I'm sorry. Dad mentioned your office and wondered what The Pearl charged for rent. He kept going on about how you must have a lot of money to afford it, and I blurted out it was rent free, compliments of Mia." Tears filled Jade's eyes. "Did he treat us to dinner because he wanted to see *us* or to grill us for information?"

"You did nothing wrong, Jade. Come here." Serena waved to her daughters. "I love you. I taught you to keep your defenses up and judge the situation. Today was a fine example." She kissed each daughter's cheek. *Mama Bear is coming for you, Justice, and you better be ready.*

Chapter Sixteen

Serena spent the night at home and got up early the next morning. Justice was at the top of her to-do list. She didn't care if he was sleeping, he would get a six-thirty call. Glad to be home, Serena went to her closet and chose a fresh outfit, showered quickly and dressed in black pants and a white blouse. She checked the mirror. "I believe this is appropriate for a prison visit."

Voices and laughter came from downstairs. School started at seven-thirty, and the twins were up and ready to go. Even though everyone was downstairs, Serena shut her bedroom door so her family wouldn't hear. "Where's my phone?"

After touching the call symbol, a groggy man's voice on the other end answered. "Hello?"

"Justice, what do you think you're doing? If you plan to be in the girls' life, don't alienate them. They realized your friendly outing was to ask them questions. This mama bear does not like it. Not one bit." Serena took a cleansing breath. "One more thing. All your smooth talking and treating them to shakes and burgers doesn't change a thing. They are loyal to me. *Me.* The parent who raised them and is always there for them. Don't ever do that again."

"Serena, you woke me up. Give me a minute." Justice paused. "Okay, I'm sorry. I was curious."

"Did you ever hear the saying, 'Curiosity killed the cat.'?"

"First you compare me to a kids' book and now sayings?"

"My dad loved sayings," Serena huffed. "Whatever. You hurt the girls. They thought you wanted to see them, not pepper them with questions about me."

"I need to learn about your lives. Since you won't go out with me, I asked the girls. I never meant to mislead them. I'll make it up to them. I promise."

"Leave them alone for a while. If you try to speak with them now, you might get rejected."

"Ouch, I really blew up our day."

"Yes, but you're accepting responsibility. It's a step in the right direction."

"Okay, I learned a lesson, Serena. You don't need to tell me I screwed up. I've heard it from my mom for six years."

Gloria is on my side? Who knew? "You should listen to her. I bet she misses the girls."

"She'd like to see them more."

"Then that's where you start. Offer to take the girls to see their grandmother," Serena replied. "And stay out of my business. Stop asking questions. Focus on Jade and Jewel. You may turn into a wonderful dad without realizing it."

"Thanks for the advice. I'm going about this all wrong. Can I call you occasionally for help and guidance?"

"Maybe." Serena checked the time. "I'm glad we had this talk, Justice. We're in our forties now. Time to grow up, which doesn't mean you still can't have fun. I'm hanging up now. I've got things to do." She ended the call and went downstairs, hoping her mom had cooked a big breakfast.

"Is that bacon I smell?" Serena asked, entering the kitchen. The girls sat at the island with a breakfast bar and a water bottle. She tapped the granite countertop and said, "You don't know what you're missing."

"It smells good," Jewel said. "But, I'm fine." She held up the bar.

"So am I." Jade repeated the gesture.

"Since you're here, I made us breakfast," Robin said. "I can't tempt the girls as hard as I try, but I know you'll eat what I've cooked."

"You can't stop me from eating one of your home-cooked meals." Serena peeked over her mom's shoulder. "Are those pancakes?"

"Of course. Made from scratch. How would you like your eggs?"

* * * *

"You lied, Teddy." Serena folded her arms and leaned back in the chair. "According to Jonathan, you came to the bar Saturday morning and ordered a bottle of champagne and one glass."

Teddy jumped from his seat, the handcuffs chaining him to the table clanked against it. "He's the liar."

"Now we have two liars," Serena stated. "Who do I believe?"

"Me!" Teddy exclaimed, sinking back into his chair. His cheeks had turned crimson red, and his eyes widened to the point Serena thought they may pop. "We're friends, Serena. You said you'd help me."

"Friends for a few days, Teddy. I've known Jonathan just as long."

"And you believe him over me?" Teddy lightly banged his forehead on the table.

"No, and will you stop that? It's making me uncomfortable."

Teddy looked up and smiled. "You care. You're still on my side."

"I'm on no one's side. Just searching for the truth."

"What about security cameras? Have the police checked the footage?" Teddy asked.

"I'll speak with Jack if I can find him. He's busy." Serena closed her eyes and exhaled. "Probably deciding if he should let you go or file formal charges. They can't hold you much longer." She opened her eyes. "I've got an idea." She dashed off a text to Lily. *Are there security cameras in the bar?*

"Did you ever think of becoming a detective instead of an author?" Teddy asked. "You have a flair for it."

"Compliments won't help your cause, Teddy. Evidence will. Besides, I'm happy with what I do."

"No more writer's block? After what happened this weekend, you've got enough for two books. Will I be in it?"

He's charming, and I hope he's found not guilty. But as Jack pointed out, I must remain objective. "I don't write about actual people," Serena answered. "I get ideas from the real world but embellish the story."

"Oh, I see." Teddy nodded. "I *am* in it."

Serena chuckled. "You wish." She folded her arms and stared at Teddy. "There's still one question you haven't answered. If you're innocent, why drug me and run? I still haven't forgiven you for that, although I slept well and the dreams…?" She waved her hand in the air, then slapped it on the table. "Well?"

"Fear is a great motivator, Serena," Teddy hung his head. "I'm sorry. With my drug history, I thought they'd charge me. I was right."

Serena's phone pinged. "I got an answer." She read Lily's message. *The hotel places security cameras in the main areas. They positioned one at the bar's entrance but not inside. What can I do to help?*

"Well?" Teddy leaned toward her.

"No cameras in the bar, but the one outside captures people entering and exiting. The Pearl had reserved the bar for the models and Mia's staff, so reviewing the footage may take time. If you entered with a group of people, it might be challenging to pinpoint your location."

"Or prove I didn't go in the bar." Teddy lifted the hand not chained to the table. "One idea down the drain."

"Don't give up so fast," Serena said. "Lily is good at what she does. Give her a chance. In the meantime, I'm going to talk to Jack." She shook her head slowly. "I pray you didn't do this, Teddy."

"I swear, Serena, I didn't." Teddy cried, blinking away tears. "No matter what happens, I'll always remember you as a friend. A good friend. One who didn't give up on me."

Serena's heart melted, yet she hadn't budged on her decision. She needed more proof, and with any luck, Lily would find the answer. "Thanks, Teddy. This may sound cliché, but I hope to see you on the outside."

Serena knocked on the door, indicating she was ready to exit. "Is Detective Ando in the building?" She asked the officer as she stepped into the hallway.

"Yes, he is meeting with Detective Mitchell now. Would you like me to give him a message?"

"Please tell him I'm here and will wait in the lobby." Serena pointed down the hall. "Which way do I go?"

"Lobby is down this hall, then turn left."

"Where is Detective Mitchell's office?"

The officer gestured in the other direction. "That way."

"The first door on the right?"

The officer gave a nod in response as a call came in. "We need you to escort a new inmate to his cell," the dispatcher said.

The officer pressed a button and spoke into the radio attached to her shoulder. "Copy that," she said, and hurried down the corridor.

Serena watched until the woman was out of sight. She didn't trust the officer to deliver the message, so she headed for Mitchell's office. When she reached her destination, she heard Jack's voice and stopped outside the door.

"You're going to book Lewis on murder charges?" Jack sounded angry. "You didn't let me finish my investigation."

"Jack, we're partners here. You and I both know he did it. I'd like to close the case."

"For the commissioner's sake?"

"He wants it wrapped up quickly."

"I know Nina Takeda, Bill. She wants justice, not a quick resolve."

"There you go again. Throwing around names. If I may remind you, you only work part-time at the station. Heaven knows how you got the job. I'm working around the clock to solve this case."

"And I'm not? It's only a part-time job when I'm not involved in a case. Then it becomes my main focus."

Serena made her move. "There you are, Jack. The officer told me I'd find you here." She faced Bill. "Hello, Detective. It appears you are hard at work on the case. I only need Jack for a minute if it's alright."

"Sure. I have paperwork to finish."

Once outside the room, Serena asked, "Is there somewhere we can talk in private?"

"I feel we keep missing each other, and you want to tell me something," Jack replied, opening a door to another detective's office. "Steve won't mind if we use his room."

"Do you remember our conversation from yesterday?" Serena asked after Jack closed the door.

"Yes, you said Jonathan had given you new information about Ted Lewis."

"It will make Bill's case stronger," Serena said. "Sorry, I overheard."

The corner of Jack's mouth twitched. "Of course, you did."

"I wasn't spying," Serena defended herself. "Bill spoke so loud I heard him halfway down the hall." She blinked, trying to appear innocent. "During your interview with Jonathan, did he ever mention Teddy coming to the bar on Saturday morning?"

Jack wrinkled his brow. "No, I've gone over my notes more than once. I found nothing."

"Have you told Bill yet? Is it the reason he wants to charge Teddy?"

"I told him, Serena. It's evidence. I didn't think he'd arrest the guy and close the case. After my meeting with Bill, I planned to return to The Pearl to speak with Jonathan."

"May I go with you?"

"Can I stop you?" Jack lifted a brow.

* * * *

They found Jonathan working at the bar. His eyebrows arched in surprise when he noticed Serena and Jack approaching.

"Hey, Jonathan," Serena said, sliding onto a stool. "It's time to tell Jack what you told me."

"Like?"

"Let's cut the act," Jack smirked. "If Ted Lewis asked you for a bottle of champagne and a glass on Saturday morning, did it slip your mind during our interview?"

Jonathan avoided his gaze. "Maybe. Did you even ask if he was here?"

"I asked for the names of everyone who ordered champagne from you. His name wasn't on the list."

"Sorry, I forgot *one* name."

"Since your memory has improved," Jack said. "Any witnesses to back up your story?"

"Models, but most have checked out of the hotel."

"Names? They have cell phones. I can call them."

"Sure, but I don't know their last names."

"Again, easy to find out," Serena said.

"Ok." Jonathan counted on his fingers. "Scarlett, Harper, Aurora…"

"Aurora? The model who twisted her ankle at rehearsal?" Serena asked. "She hobbled in here on Saturday?"

"Yeah, in a walking boot and sat right at that table." Jonathan pointed to one close to the bar.

"Go on," Jack said. "Anyone else?"

"Natalie."

"Natalie Grey, the plus-size model?" Serena stopped taking notes. "I haven't seen her in days."

"Trust me, she's here," Jack said under his breath.

"Natalie comes in late at night to drink," Jonathan answered. "The poor girl is depressed. She spends most of her time in her room."

"I'll meet up with her tonight." Serena addressed Jack before shifting her attention to Jonathan. "What time does she come in?"

"Around ten. Stays till midnight. The witching hour she calls it."

"If you remember anything else, I suggest you contact me," Jack said, laying his card on the countertop.

"You know where to find me, Detective." Jonathan pointed to the ground. "Behind this bar."

Chapter Seventeen

Arriving at the bar at ten p.m. sharp, Serena found Jonathan and Natalie deep in conversation. While they might be mistaken for a loving couple by some, Serena suspected them of conspiracy. Recent discoveries supported her theory.

The duo hadn't noticed her, so Serena sat out of view and opened her journal and wrote: *The police suspect Jonathan and Natalie of a crime. What if they teamed up to frame Teddy? If one was guilty, the innocent person unwittingly helps the other go free. If Teddy did or didn't murder Ava, they could manufacture evidence to make sure he's convicted and divert attention from themselves.* She glanced around the room, watching people enjoy their evening. *Is that fair? No, but it makes a great story.*

Her initial thoughts about the crime had taken a sudden turn. Nothing seemed as it should. *Time to get a drink.*

Serena strolled up to the bar and placed her purse next to Natalie. "Hi, Natalie. Glad you're here. We can have happy hour. No fun drinking alone."

"Serena, I'm glad to see a friendly face," Natalie said. "Jonathan and I were saying we can't wait for this investigation to end."

"From what I've heard, it should wrap up soon."

"Ooh, do tell. You have connections we don't."

"I shouldn't. After all, you're still suspects." Serena grimaced, hoping they'd fall for her hesitance.

"Please," Natalie begged.

"If you promise not to reveal your source," Serena said.

"We won't," they said simultaneously. Jonathan surprised Serena by flashing the three-fingered scout salute.

"The police have a good case against Ted Lewis." Serena sucked air into her mouth. "No, I can't. It's too awful."

"What?" Natalie asked.

Serena lowered her head and whispered, "They are formally charging him with the crime. It may have already happened."

"Does Detective Ando still need my statement?" Jonathan asked.

"I believe so, but I'm not the police," Serena answered. She faced Natalie. "Jack may want to speak with you, too."

"Why? I did nothing wrong."

"Can you confirm Jonathan's story? You saw Ted Lewis come into the bar on Saturday morning."

"Oh, yeah, that. Yes, I can."

"Then Jack will want a statement. The police are still checking security footage, and Jack is calling the models from your list, Johnathan." Serena observed their faces, and their expressions never changed.

"Let me get you a drink, Serena. Gin and tonic, right?" Jonathan grabbed a bottle, and Serena watched him pour the gin. He squirted from the hose, which held the washes, chose a lime and set the glass in front of her. "On me."

"Thanks. Care to sit at a table, Natalie?"

"Sure. Pick one out, and I'll be there in a minute."

This time, Serena chose a table close to the bar. She wasn't surprised to see the bartender and the model almost jovial in their actions. While she waited, Serena sent a P.I.C. message to her friends along with the word, breakfast.

"You made my day," Natalie said as she took the seat across from Serena. "Or should I say night? Ted Lewis is going down."

"Shh. Someone might hear," Serena hissed. "Wait for it to become public knowledge." She exhaled. "I feel sorry for Teddy. He's a broken man."

"You've seen him?"

"I visited him at the jail."

"Did he confess to you?" Natalie said, lowering her voice.

"No, just the opposite. He gave me reasons why he's not guilty." Serena paused. "But Detective Mitchell is determined to close the investigation. He feels he's got enough evidence after Jack spoke with Jonathan. All they need is a formal statement."

"When Mia gave you access to the event, did you expect something like this to happen? Great material for your book, right?" Natalie widened her eyes. "It never occurred to me that something so dreadful could happen at an exclusive fashion show. This was my first job. Mia gave me a chance of a lifetime." She sighed. "Now what?"

"Like you, I never imagined something terrible would occur." Serena shook her head. "Am I thinking of my book right now? Absolutely not. People and relationships outweigh material possessions or financial pursuits. I'm committed to this case and intend to see it through to its end. When I met Jonathan, Teddy and you, I felt a connection. I like each one of you but must not let it cloud my judgment."

"Do the police like that you're involved in the case?"

"Probably not, but how can they stop me? I try to keep a low profile while collecting evidence. If it's credible, I send it to Jack." Serena sipped her drink. "Enough about the case. Let's talk about you. Boyfriend? Or is Jonathan your new love interest?"

"No boyfriend. Jonathan is great, but he's a…"

"Bartender?"

Natalie grimaced. "No offense, but he's twenty-nine and working behind the bar. It's his only job."

"Maybe The Pearl pays well or he's looking for advancement."

Natalie lifted her shoulder. "You make a valid point, but I'm not staying to find out. I'll head back to New York once I'm cleared."

"Do you live in the city? It's quite expensive."

"I live with three roommates. A struggling artist, a screenwriter, and an actor. They're fun, creative people. Add in the model and you have a sitcom."

"Are you in contact with your roommates? The screenwriter could use your situation for a play or series," Serena said, half-teasing.

"How did you know?" Natalie giggled. "Why am I asking? Of course, you did. You're creative, too. Don't steal the idea."

"Never, unless I moved in with you." Serena smiled, yet she wondered what game Natalie played. *Is Natalie vying for her fifteen minutes of fame? She wants to be noticed so her roommate can pitch his script with her name attached to it. The model who was suspected of murder. No, it's too farfetched. How would he know this would happen?*

"Are you planning to move to New York?" Natalie joked.

"Not anytime soon." From her vantage point, Serena had a clear view of the entrance and casually observed the people entering the bar. One man seemed familiar. He stopped, placed his hands on his hips and scanned the room as if searching for someone. She blinked to clear her vision, not sure of who she saw. *Justice?* "No, please, no." She placed her forehead in her hand and peeked under her fingers.

It took less than a minute for her ex to locate her. Justice lifted his hand in greeting. "Serena."

"Am I missing something?" Natalie checked over her shoulder. "Is it that hot guy waving at you?"

"Yes, my ex-husband. Thanks for thinking he's hot."

"You're welcome. It's also my cue to go. I'll be at the bar if you need me." Natalie pushed her seat back as Justice arrived. He helped with her chair, and she thanked him.

"Don't leave on my account," Justice said, giving her his best smile.

"I'm not. Please, take my seat." Natalie wiggled her fingers at Serena and walked to the bar.

Serena dug her nails into her palms. "How did you know where to find me?"

"It wasn't hard. Besides working here, I discovered you have a suite in the hotel. When the desk rang your room, and you didn't answer, I decided to explore. It's past eleven. Where else would you be?"

"I was visiting friends," Serena stated and rose from her seat. "Now I'm going to my room."

"Wait," Justice pleaded. "Don't go."

"Fine," Serena huffed, dropping back into her chair. "I will stay so you can ask *me* your prying questions instead of the girls."

Justice winced. "Are they still upset with me?"

"Give them time. They're teenagers. They'll get over it."

"Remember when we met, Serena? We were teenagers, the same age as the twins."

"They're smarter than I was. We got married too young, which proved to be a big mistake."

"I don't agree. You were my girl, and I wanted to put a ring on your finger. I have no regrets."

"You still don't see, do you? You failed to grow with the family, Justice, and kept living the same lifestyle." Her heart ached for him, and Serena understood why he felt that way. He wanted to embrace the past and keep it alive, but they couldn't recreate it.

Serena wished to reach out and touch Justice's cheek, stroke his fine beard to comfort him but was afraid he'd take it the wrong way. She'd made her decision about their relationship, and nothing could change her mind. *I'll reminisce, but I won't go back to you. I see a bright future for me and girls, and you aren't part of my plan. The girls, yes, but me, no.*

"I can change," Justice whispered.

"No." Serena shook her head. "You can't." She could tell he didn't like her answer and switched to another subject. "Ask your questions."

"Fine, I see you don't want to discuss our situation." Justice ran his hand over his head, a habit Serena recognized from their time together. It helped him think before he spoke. "First, I want to say it's cool you have an office and suite at The Pearl. Your book was an instant success. You probably thought it was the reason I contacted you. I'll admit I was jealous, but when I thought about it, I discovered it wasn't jealousy which consumed me, but regret. I made mistakes and wished I was on the journey with you."

"If we stayed together, I wouldn't have become a rideshare driver and met Mia," Serena replied.

"Mia." Justice hung his head. "She seems like a good friend."

"She is. Mia wants what is best for me," Serena said, then looked straight at Justice. "I don't care about her money."

"I believe you, Serena. You get along with everyone. People still ask me about you."

"It's nice to hear." Serena smiled. "Anything else you want to know? The Takedas are friends. I have a free office and suite at The Pearl. I wrote a bestseller and still drive for my rideshare company. That about covers it."

"You always were a dynamo and could handle two tasks at once. I remember one time you had Jade on one hip and Jewel on the other and opened the refrigerator with your chin." Justice slapped his leg and chuckled.

"While you watched," Serena said in a deadpan voice.

"It was too good to interfere, babe."

"Thanks for the reminder." Serena seethed, recalling the many times Justice said, "You got this," when it came to the girls or chores. "Let me ask *you* a question," she said, before he remembered any more stories that he found humorous, and she didn't. "Do you have a girlfriend?"

"Ah…" Justice tapped his chin. "For the moment."

"What does that mean?"

"Um…"

"You have a girlfriend!" Serena jumped to her feet. Although she didn't care, the lying caused anger to rise inside her. "You asked me to marry you. Does she know that?"

Justice stood to block her path and grasped Serena's wrist. "Babe."

"Don't 'babe' me." Serena struggled to release his grip.

"Is everything alright here?" Jack's voice came from behind Serena.

"Detective Ando," Justice said, letting Serena go. "Good to see you unwind with a drink after a long day."

"I asked if everything is alright here," Jack repeated.

"Sure, the wife and I…"

"I'm not your wife," Serena said through gritted teeth.

"Were having a slight disagreement," Justice continued. "About what day we should get married."

"I see." Jack appeared confused, then faced Serena. "Sorry, I had no idea." He strode to the exit before Serena could answer.

"Jack, wait." Despite wanting to hurl every derogatory name at Justice, her focus remained on Jack.

Pursuing him, Serena increased her stride to close the gap between them. She found herself jogging to close the distance. Jack had already reached the elevators when she finally caught up with him. "Jack," Serena said, catching her breath. "Please give me a chance to explain."

"You had a date." Jack narrowed his eyes. "Nothing to explain."

"No, I didn't. Justice came to the hotel and searched until he found me. Trust me, I was just as surprised as you were. I'd only gone to the bar to find Natalie. Jonathan said she usually arrived around ten. I intended to speak with her in a casual setting, hoping she'd be more relaxed."

"Justice said you're getting married."

"No way! He was trying to get you to leave. He wanted to make you angry, and it worked." Serena slipped her hand into Jack's and squeezed. "Were you looking for me?"

"Yes."

Serena questioned if she felt a squeeze in return. "Did you..." She pointed with her other hand to their clasped ones.

"Maybe."

"Let's clear the air. I'm single and do not plan to remarry or date or fill in the blank my ex-husband."

"That's pretty clear."

"Good." Serena gave one nod of the head. "If you see us together, we are discussing the twins or I'm telling him we're never getting back together."

"Got it."

"Do you?" Serena stepped in front of him. She placed her palms on his muscled chest, tilted her head back and gazed into his dreamy brown eyes. "You are amazing, did you know that?" she whispered.

Jack's lips found hers, and their sweet kiss deepened into a passionate one. His arms slipped around her, and he gripped her firmly, yet gently if that was possible. Serena's head spun with happiness. Jack might be the one.

Chapter Eighteen

"It was an eventful day," Serena announced to her friends as she examined the breakfast menu. The tearoom offered a selection of quiches, breakfast breads and bagels. She finally made her choice and told the server, "I'll have the broccoli cheddar quiche with banana bread, please."

"Anything else?" the woman asked the table.

"We're good," Mia answered, then waited for her to leave. "Now," she said, locking eyes with Serena. "What happened last night?"

"During my visit to the bar, I found Jonathan and Natalie leaning toward each other and whispering. In my opinion, they are planning to frame Teddy."

"Sounds like conspiracy or love," Lily said.

"It's the first one, Lily. Conspiracy. I asked Natalie if she was in a relationship or if she liked Jonathan. She confirmed what I suspected. No significant other, and she considers Jonathan's' job a deal breaker."

Lily leaned back in her chair. "Whoa. Okay."

"I'm not finished," Serena said with a sigh. "Around eleven, Justice makes an unexpected appearance and proposes, even though he has a girlfriend. Then, I kissed Jack."

Mia, who'd been scrolling on her iPad, glanced up and said, "Hold on. Did I hear you say you kissed Jack?"

"Justice has a girlfriend?" Lily exclaimed. "And still asked you to marry him?"

"Yes, to all." Serena grinned. "What a day."

"No kidding! How was the kiss?" Mia asked.

"Wonderful." Serena suddenly felt protective of her budding romance. "We're taking things slow."

"How did the kiss happen?" Lily wrinkled her nose. "Did Justice leave, and Jack appear?'

Serena summed up the night, enjoying the expressions on her friends' faces. "Do you think I made my intentions clear to Jack?'

"Oh, the kiss sealed it," Mia said with a laugh. She became serious as she held up her iPad. "The local news headline for today."

Serena read aloud, "Famed photographer Ted Lewis charged with supermodel's murder. Oh, no. Bill went ahead with his threat. Jack had asked for more time." She faced Lily. "Have you gone through the footage?"

"It's running as we speak. I set facial recognition to auto, and it hasn't generated any hits on Ted Lewis. The parts I watched showed many people entering and exiting the bar. Some were in groups. Some alone. I never saw Ted."

"If you don't find him, does it prove Teddy wasn't there?" Serena asked.

"One hundred percent? No, but he can use it as evidence with The Pearl's permission," Lily stated. "You still believe he's innocent, Serena?"

"Most of me does." Serena hung her head. "Since the police have charged Teddy, will they clear Jonathan and Natalie? She wants to go back to New York. I need to step up my investigation before she does. One of the three is guilty, and today is the day to unravel the truth."

"How can I help?" Mia asked.

"If Natalie gets the okay to leave, can you delay her? Sign her to another show? Act interested in her career?" Serena poured another cup of tea and inhaled the scent.

"I'll check the security feed every fifteen minutes," Lily said. "Let's stay in touch throughout the day. Where do you plan to start, Serena?"

"Where I do my best work. My office. I need more background on these three people. They told me their stories, but are they true? If I am going to become an investigator, I need to act like one. The police don't release someone merely based on their claim of innocence. They need evidence. Facts. I looked at this the wrong way. I'm not at a casual tea party, engaging in small talk or listening to personal anecdotes. It goes beyond that."

"You've thought this through," Mia said. "It will help your writing, too."

"Especially when I write *High Heels and High Stakes.*"

"Is that the title?" Mia asked.

"Do you like it?"

"Yes, much better than *The Model's Murder*." Mia giggled.

Lily nodded. "I approve." She took her last bite of quiche and drank her tea to the bottom. "I'm going downstairs to work in the security offices. They may point me in a direction we've missed. I won't leave the hotel unless circumstances dictate, but I'll let you know if I do."

"Same for me," Mia replied. "I've got a lot on my schedule today. If you hear the police have cleared Natalie, and she can leave the hotel, text me immediately."

Before departing, Serena cast a glance around the room, savoring the tranquil atmosphere. The calming green color brought her peace, and no matter what went on outside these walls, it helped start her day.

The women walked down the flagstone path, parting at the koi pond. Serena checked her handbag for the special honey oat cereal for Samurai. They were long overdue for a talk. She rested her arms on the fence's top railing and shook the bag. "Sam?" she called.

Beautiful orange koi with black patterns and white koi with red or orange spots swam past underwater. Serena studied each one, but not one looked like Sam. *It's not that big of a pond. Did something happen to him?* Serena panicked and dug for her phone. She dialed Nina's number.

"Serena?" Nina answered on the first ring.

"Yes, it's me. Nina, I can't find Samurai."

"I know."

"You know and didn't tell me? He died?"

"Oh, no, my child. Samurai is getting his health check-up. He should return to the pond soon."

"Could you find out when?"

"Certainly. Hold on." Serena counted the minutes until Nina came back online. "You still there?" she asked.

"Yes. Did Sam pass his tests?"

"With flying colors. He's on his way back to the pond."

Serena placed a hand over her racing heart. "Thank you, Nina."

"I'll talk to you soon, Serena. Stay safe."

Serena walked over to the bench to wait. She planned to witness the return of Samurai and his placement back in the pond.

A man and woman, carrying a clear tank between them, approached the fence surrounding the water and unlocked the gate. They wore high boots and stepped with proficiency into the pond. Using caution, they lowered the tank into the water and slid up a door, allowing the fish to swim out and join the rest. Once the koi departed the tank, they pushed the door into place.

The woman handed the man a net, and he searched for specific fish. Serena watched in awe as he chose four koi and skillfully placed them in the tank. The man hoisted the container up to the surface while the woman pushed from the water. They guided the tank onto dry land and left as quietly as they had come.

A familiar red face surfaced, and Serena cried with joy. *Why am I so happy? He's a fish.* "I heard you got a clean bill of health. Congrats."

Sam swam in circles, then returned to his spot. His mouth opened and closed as if questioning why Serena had come. She strolled to the fence and tossed a few oats his way. "I've got to solve the case today, Sam. Did you see the headlines?" *Why am I assuming he read the news?* "The police accused Teddy of the crime, and according to Bill Mitchell, case closed."

The fish appeared to move his head in an up and down fashion. "Don't give up?" Serena leaned over the railing and pointed at him. "Are you nodding or am I hallucinating?"

The red koi appeared to smile at her. He swam underwater and popped up to the surface. "Let me ask you something, Sam. Did Teddy ever come here and talk to the fish?" Serena recalled how Sam had shown her heads or tails to answer her. "Heads for yes. Tails for no."

The fish kept his head above water. "Did he mention Ava's death?" Serena asked. "Your head is still above water, so yes. Was he afraid the police would suspect him?" *Head is still up.* She decided to go for it. "Did Ted say he killed Ava?"

Immediately, Sam dove into the water, and his white tail appeared above water.

"Okay, I see how this works. One more. This is a trick question. Did Ted say he didn't kill Ava, and you believe him?"

Sam disappeared and popped up twice.

"No, this can't be happening. I'm conversing with a fish. To top it off, I believe him. Teddy is not guilty.

Thanks, Sam." Serena tossed the entire bag of oats into the water so Sam and his friends could enjoy the snack. "I've got some research to do. See you later."

✶ ✶ ✶ ✶

Even though the stakes were high, the office felt friendly and familiar. The quiet atmosphere would help her work. Serena sat in front of her computer screen, ready to take a deep dive into each suspect's life. "I'll start with Teddy." She typed his name into the search engine, finding the highlights of his career and his drug use on the first page.

The man's details took a different turn on page four. Her heart skipped a beat as she read: *Photographer spends free time snapping photos then donating them to families at children's hospitals.* Tears welled in her eyes, and Serena printed the page. "I can do more than print this. Someone needs to see it."

Serena texted Jack, asking for his work email. It only took a minute before she received a response. She copied the website address and pasted it into a blank email. After adding Jack's address, she sent it off, hoping he'd read the email when it arrived.

"This proves Teddy is a good man." Serena gestured to the screen. "He offered to give me photos of the girls free of charge. Now I see why. He uses his skills to help others."

When she'd reached the tenth page, Serena halted her search. She'd find no additional details that would help or hurt Teddy.

A text from Lily distracted her, and she reached for her phone. "Let's see what you discovered, Lily." She read the message. "The security team suggested I add Natalie into the face recognition auto search. So far, it hasn't found her. Strange. Didn't she say she was there?"

"Interesting." Serena returned a text, answering the question. "Yes, she said she saw Teddy." She returned to her computer screen, closed the window and opened a new one. "On to the next person. Jonathan."

Serena had already read Jonathan's work file, yet she needed details about his everyday life. *Will a search bring anything to light?* Social media had the answers. It appeared Jonathan was quite active on three sites, posting pictures with models from this weekend and partying with friends throughout the years.

Checking the dated posts, Serena could tell when Jonathan had someone in his life and when he didn't. "No girlfriend in the picture now." She leaned back and stared at the ceiling. "What do these sites tell me? He's immature. Likes to brag. He looks good without a shirt." *Is Jonathan that shallow?*

Serena drummed her fingers on the pile of books she kept near her. If someone in the hotel wanted a signed copy, she'd pull one from the stack and give it to the staff to deliver. If the fan was close to her office, she could readily hand them one. She patted the books. *That's it. Books. Is Jonathan smarter than he's letting on? Does that make him cold and calculating? He lets people think he's the tan, blonde guy who loves to party. Yet British crime series are his favorite. He likes to read. He asked for a signed copy of my book.*

"And you shall get one." Taking a paperback from the pile, Serena signed the book and headed for the bar.

* * * *

When Serena entered the room, she discovered two women behind the bar. She scanned the area in search of Jonathan. Approaching one bartender, she greeted her with a friendly, "Hi" and asked, "Is Jonathan here?"

"You just missed him," she answered. "He got word he's cleared of all charges and went to his room to pack."

"Do you know the room number?"

"No, sorry, and if I did, I couldn't' give it to you."

"It's okay." Serena dashed off a text to Nina before the woman finished her sentence.

Nina's answer arrived promptly. "He's in the employee wing. Room 10. Lower level."

Serena thought she'd double-check the location, so she asked the bartender, "Is room ten in the basement?"

"How did you get his room number?"

"Helps to know people. Well?"

"Yes, there's a wing with free rooms when employees need them. A perk of the job. Not the best view." She smiled. "But a comfortable bed and nice décor."

"Thanks." Serena rushed for the elevators, pushed the button and tapped her foot. "I need to text Mia. I'm certain they cleared Natalie, too." She typed a brief message, barely able to hit the keys with her trembling fingers.

Upon hearing an elevator's arrival, Serena searched the hallway to determine which one. The doors slid back on the farthest one, and Jonathan stepped from the cubicle. "Serena! Come to send me off?"

"No." Serena held up her book. "I came to deliver this. I promised."

"Cool." Jonathan approached her, carrying a duffel bag. He set in on the floor and unzipped it. "I can say I know the author, too. Thanks." Jonathan slipped the book into the bag.

"Mind if I walk with you?" Serena asked.

"It's a short one, but sure."

"When did the police contact you?"

"Late morning. They said they had cleared me of any wrongdoing, and I could leave the hotel. When Audrey and Candice arrived for their shift, I went downstairs and showered." Jonathan lifted his bag. "My friend had thrown some clothes in here, and I needed to pack."

"Where's home?"

"I rent in Hayes Valley. It's a great place to live. Lots of bars, restaurants, parks, coffee shops."

"Yeah, I know," Serena answered. "I live here, too."

"I guess I forgot." Jonathan laughed.

"Before you go," Serena said with a loud exhale of breath. "I hesitate to ask, but did you lie about Teddy coming into the bar on Saturday?"

"Why would I lie?"

"To save yourself. Take the heat off you and put it on Teddy. You're the bartender. So many people come in and out of the bar. You could justify your lie by saying you made a mistake."

A deep red color traveled up Jonathan's neck, almost reaching his cheeks. "So? I didn't commit the crime, and I was tired of answering questions."

"What about Natalie? You said she was a witness and could back up your story."

"No, she never came into the bar on Saturday." Jonathan shook his head, appearing guilty. "She agreed to help me."

"Or you agreed to help each other?"

"Maybe, but it's over. The police found their man. They charged Ted Lewis with the crime."

Chapter Nineteen

Serena couldn't type fast enough as they walked through the lobby. She messaged Jack that she'd gotten the truth from Jonathan. She ended with, "You need to stop Jonathan from leaving the hotel. He admits to conspiring with Natalie."

"Hey, are you always working?" Jonathan gestured to her phone.

"Sorry. Sending myself a to-do list."

"Hope one of them is to start your book."

"How did you know?" Serena teased.

"Lucky guess?" Jonathan shrugged. "So this is it," he said when they arrived at the hotel's entrance. "Wish I got to know you under better circumstances."

Serena forced a smile. "Yeah, we may have become friends."

Jonathan held out his arms, and Serena compelled her body to move in his direction. *Am I in the arms of a killer?* "Stay safe, Jonathan." *And may Jack stop you before you get too far.*

Jonathan stepped back and took Serena by the shoulders. "Why do we act like this is our last encounter? I work here, and so do you."

Serena laughed. "What were we thinking?" *That I wouldn't visit you behind bars.*

"My ride is here," Jonathan said. "See you around."

Serena watched the scene unfold from the lobby. A police car with flashing lights pulled into the curved driveway and blocked the path of outgoing cars. Jonathan backed away as two officers jumped out and headed for him. A portion of her filled with compassion as they escorted Jonathan to the back seat of their vehicle. "Tell the truth," she whispered.

Serena's phone pinged twice. *Two messages?* She read Mia's first. "I asked Natalie to meet me for lunch. We're in the dining room. Join us." Then she moved on to Jack's. "Did they get there in time?"

Torn over what to do, Serena headed for a safe place. After arriving at her office, she went straight for her chair. "I haven't started Natalie's background check, so I can't join them for lunch without more information. Before I begin, I must answer Jack." She typed one word, "Yes!"

Serena's hands hovered over the keyboard. Despite finding Jonathan's information on social media, she fought the temptation. "Start each search the same way."

Entering 'Natalie Grey' into the search engine, Serena waited on the results. Natalie had not modeled before Mia's show, so Serena found little about her fashion career.

No modeling articles or photos surfaced on any page. Eventually, she gave in and searched social media sites.

"Should have looked here first," Serena mumbled. She studied every photo of the model, hunting for clues. It seemed Natalie stayed in touch with her high school cheerleader friends, due to all the throwback pictures. "A cheerleader? Makes no sense. Hmm, this post says college is not for her, and she dropped out after sophomore year. Was modeling her passion?"

More recent posts touched on her life in New York City. Natalie posed in the middle of Times Square and with other landmarks. Serena wondered if she was doing a practice photo shoot. "Wait a minute." She slammed her palm on the desk. "Most models are discovered early, in their teen years. They aren't cheerleaders. What was Natalie thinking?"

Scrolling through more posts, one caused Serena to come to an abrupt halt. The photographer had caught Natalie celebrating midair. "Only twenty pounds to go!" Serena read. She tapped her chin. "Natalie was losing weight?" She stared at the picture, trying to guess her size. "No. It's just the opposite. She is trying to gain weight to become a plus-size model. The girl will do anything to break into the fashion world."

Serena returned to the photos she had skipped, starting from January of the previous year. "Since it's winter, Natalie is wearing coats outside. I need a picture taken indoors."

After finding one she liked, Serena printed the photo. "On to spring." She kept repeating the process until she reached January of this year.

Placing the photos in order, Serena studied the changes in Natalie. By the holidays, she appeared to have gained weight. Serena compared her size to Natalie's. *It's hard to tell from a picture. I'd guess size ten. This makes no sense. She needed to gain enough weight in two months to wear size sixteen.* "I think it's time for lunch."

* * * *

A server escorted Serena to Mia's table. "One more for lunch?" she asked.

"Yes, thank you," Serena answered, sitting next to Natalie.

"Serena!" Natalie exclaimed.

"I thought I'd surprise you," Mia said. "It seems you and Serena became friends, and you'd want to say goodbye."

"I do." Natalie patted Serena's hand.

"When is your flight?" Serena asked.

Natalie gestured to Mia. "Mia has graciously offered to fly me home on the Takeda jet. Do you believe it?"

Serena glanced across the table to see Mia lift an eyebrow. "Yes, when it comes to helping people, Mia is generous."

"We can enjoy our lunch and not worry about missing a flight," Mia replied.

Up close and in the daylight, Serena noticed a bead of sweat along Natalie's top lip. *Strange. It's not warm in the restaurant. Maybe she's overly excited.*

"Mia may hire me for her next show," Natalie said. "*If I'm available.*"

Serena met Mia's eyes and bit her lip. "Your career has officially started," she said. "If I remember correctly, this was your first show."

Natalie looked down at her hands and folded them. "Yes. I appreciate the opportunity."

Either she's a fantastic actress or genuinely means it. "While we wait for lunch, why don't you tell us about yourself, Natalie?"

Natalie pulled her water glass toward her and sipped through the glass straw. "There isn't much to tell. I dropped out of college when I was nineteen. It wasn't for me. I dreamed of becoming a model."

"Since you were young? Did your mom drag you to auditions?" Serena asked.

"No." Natalie's shoulders slumped. "She signed me up for every cheerleading camp she could find. She wanted to relive her past."

"Did you ever tell her you were interested in modeling?"

"When I got to high school, I got the nerve to tell her. She said it was a phase and it would pass."

"I know the feeling," Mia said. "My parents wanted me to become a doctor or research scientist. I planned to follow my own path. During my high school years, I explored all my possibilities. They didn't like it when I announced I'd go to Florida State for freshman year."

Natalie tilted her head. "Do they have a fashion program?"

Mia shook her head and smiled. "Not really. I wanted to distance myself from California and my parents. The college had a medical college and might be the reason they granted permission." She leaned forward as if to tell a secret. "I skipped a year in grade school, so I wasn't eighteen. I needed to get to my next birthday and become of age so I could make my own choices."

"Wow, you tricked your parents," Natalie said.

"In a way, yes. When I turned eighteen, I applied to fashion schools all over the country and two accepted me. Luckily, I chose the right one." Mia smiled. "It's where I met Jordan."

"You are proof that following your dreams works," Natalie replied. "It's hard, but I'm glad I did the same thing."

"And see where you are?" Serena gestured toward Mia. "Sitting at a table with a well-known fashion designer, Mia Takeda."

"Don't forget the debut author with a bestselling novel," Mia added with a giggle.

"This is the best." Natalie beamed.

A server brought salads to the table, and the women made small talk while they ate. Serena never ordered, then realized Mia had chosen the food before they arrived. A cup of tomato bisque soup came next, and she enjoyed the homemade croutons floating on top. Before the main meal came, Serena's phone rang. She glanced at the name on the screen. *Jack.*

"Is it your agent?" Mia asked.

"Yes, I must take this. Excuse me." Serena walked to a quiet spot and answered, "Jack?"

"Serena, I have new information."

"So do I, but you go first."

"I called the models on Jonathan's list. Aurora was the most helpful."

"I met her," Serena said. "She's the one who injured her ankle."

"Yes, she sprained it, and the doctor prescribed a walking boot. Aurora didn't want to miss the excitement. She sat in the bar to people watch, then moved to the hall for the fashion show. Despite being the first to arrive at the bar, she never saw Teddy enter the room."

"What about Natalie? Did Aurora see her?"

"No."

"Does this clear Teddy?"

"Almost. What did you find?"

"It's not a crime, but over the past year, Natalie has tried to gain weight to become a plus-size model."

"You're right. Not a crime." Jack chuckled.

"Are you laughing?" Serena said in mock surprise. "Detective Jack Ando found something funny?"

"What else did you discover?" Jack's voice returned to normal.

"I'm in the restaurant with Mia and Natalie. Mia offered Natalie the Takeda jet as a way of detaining her."

"Great thinking."

"We're keeping up the pretense of a girls' lunch, hoping Natalie may slip up and say something about Jonathan. Speaking of him, how is he?"

"He admitted he lied about Ted Lewis. No mention of Natalie."

"Maybe they worked together to eliminate Ava."

"No one is exonerated yet, Serena. But I think you could be right. The couple worked together in some fashion to save themselves."

"Did I hear you correctly, officer?"

"What?"

"You said I was right."

"One time, Serena, and I said you *could* be right."

"You've said I was right more than once, Jack."

"Hey, I've got to go. Keep Natalie busy for me."

"There's only so much we can eat," Serena teased.

"I've got an idea. Ask Mia to send Natalie to the spa while she waits for her flight."

"Excellent, Jack. I'll let her know. Have you visited the spa?"

"No."

"Would you go for a couple's massage?'

"Couples what?"

"Never mind. I'll put it on our to-do list."

"We have a list?" Jack exhaled.

"Oh, Jack, don't be so dramatic." Serena smiled at his cute response. "Don't you have police-things to do?"

"Yes. Once I'm done, I'll return to the hotel."

"Look forward to seeing you." Serena ended her call and sent Mia the spa message before heading for the table.

"It sounds wonderful," Natalie said to Mia as Serena sat in her designated place.

"Ooh, tell me," Serena said, pretending to be clueless.

"I'm going to have a spa day while the plane gets ready for departure," Natalie answered.

"You're right. It sounds wonderful." Serena grinned at Mia.

Two servers brought out three plates of lemon sole in a light cream sauce. Cut lemons, curled to perfection, and capers adorned the fish. A part of Serena wished for a girls' luncheon so she could enjoy the experience. As she listened to Natalie's voice, a feeling of sadness washed over her. *She doesn't know we're getting closer to the truth. Is it Natalie or Jonathan?*

Mia was the first to rise. "It's been lovely, but I've got a million things to do."

"I'll walk you out," Serena said. "Natalie, have a safe trip home."

"Thanks, and it was nice to meet you, Serena. You two go without me. I plan to order dessert." Natalie looked at Mia. "If it is okay with you."

"Sure. Enjoy." Mia took Serena's arm and strolled down the main aisle to the exit. She stopped at the check-in podium. "Whatever she wants, give it to her," she told the woman.

"Yes, Ms. Takeda." The hostess nodded.

"We did well, don't you think?" Mia asked once they stepped into the hotel's lobby.

"Natalie didn't suspect a thing. She loved every minute of our lunch," Serena answered. "Although I feel sorry for her. She's desperate to follow her dream."

"What lengths will someone go to achieve it?" Mia widened her eyes. "Murder? But there's something that bothers me. I don't see a connection between Ava and Natalie. Sure, Ava harassed her and said she shouldn't be in the show." She let out a breath. "But Ava bullied many people."

"That's it, Mia," Serena replied. "We need to discover her motive. If Natalie did harm Ava, it's the missing piece."

"This is where we part ways, my friend." Mia wrapped an arm around Serena's shoulders. "You'll reach your goal. We have several hours left in the day."

"At the stroke of midnight, I'll turn into a pumpkin if I don't solve this," Serena laughed.

Serena stopped by the hall leading to the elevators to use her phone. She needed an update from her mom and wanted to tell the girls she loved them. Leaning against the wall, she started typing, oblivious to the people passing by her.

"Serena?" a woman's voice said.

Startled, Serena pulled her eyes away from the screen.

"Didn't mean to give you a start." Ruby Sullivan, the beautiful model Serena had met on rehearsal day, touched her arm. "Sorry."

"No, I wasn't paying attention." Serena smiled. "I never expected to see you here. Most models have left the building."

"A few stayed. Mia gave us three days of free room and board plus spa privileges if we did. I always wanted to see San Francisco, so I took advantage of the offer."

I should also take advantage of this gift. "Do you have a minute?"

"Sure. I came down for a coffee."

"Let's get you one and go to my office."

"Only if I get a signed copy of your book," Ruby teased. "And make it out to my mom."

Chapter Twenty

The two women settled in Serena's office. Ruby held onto her expresso and sipped from the cup. She had insisted Serena order something, so she'd chosen iced green tea. Ruby glanced around the room observing the décor while Serena reached for a book.

"That's an interesting choice of artwork," Ruby said, pointing to Serena's suspect board.

Serena had used push pins and an old scarf to shield her work. "It's a work in progress," she joked. "What's your mom's name?"

"Adele."

Serena scribbled an inscription and handed Ruby the book. "May I ask you something?"

"Is it about me?" Ruby smiled.

"It's about Natalie. I'll understand if you don't want to talk about someone else."

"Depends on the question."

"Do the other models like her?"

"Some do. Some don't. Not anything unusual. Natalie kept to herself since she was the only plus-size."

"What about Ava? Ever see them fight?"

"No, but strangely, they avoided each other as if they were feuding."

"Any idea what started it?"

"From the gossip I heard, and mind you, it's only gossip, Ava thought Natalie had odd habits. She wouldn't let the dresser touch her and asked for privacy. Somehow, he gave in to her, which really angered Ava. It's quite unusual to hide while dressing."

Serena longed to write in her notebook yet needed to keep things casual. "Any other unusual habits?'

"Natalie stayed in her room, even before the police made her a suspect. We'd invite her to dinner or for drinks, and she always said no."

Serena recalled a conversation in the bar. She'd spoken with Natalie who had appeared upset, and Serena wanted to comfort her.

"No, I must remain in control," Natalie had said. "Everyone is your enemy. The girls are backstabbing each other, even the ones the police deemed innocent, and it's quite ugly."

"When did this happen? Not here." Serena remembered thinking it seemed cruel.

"Last night in the hotel hallway," Natalie had answered. "We're all on the same floor."

Serena mulled over the conversation. She hesitated before asking Ruby the next question. "Natalie said things got ugly on your floor. A group of models congregated in the hallway and accused each other of Ava's murder."

"What?" Ruby slapped her thigh. "Is that what she said? No way. We'd returned from a night of drinking. The police cleared many of the girls, and they wanted to celebrate. I never made the suspect list but wanted to join them."

"Did Natalie go?"

"No, she stayed in her room."

"Then how did she get involved?"

"Upon our return, we stayed in the hallway, not ready to return to our rooms. Someone said, 'You killed Ava,' like 'tag, you're it'. It sounds terrible when I say it now, but some women were quite drunk. It turned into a silly game, and one girl pounded on Natalie's door and screamed it. The sober people stopped all the nonsense before it got worse. Maybe that's what Natalie meant when she said it got ugly. I viewed it as girls blowing off steam. It had been an intense couple of days."

"Thanks for your help," Serena said. "I won't keep you any longer. What's on your sightseeing list for today?"

"I may go to an art museum. Some girls aren't interested, but I hope a few will join me." Ruby stood and held up the book. "Thanks for this." She walked out the door using a strut any model would envy.

"Hope your mom enjoys the book," Serena said under her breath.

* * * *

Serena's mind spun with the new information. *What's up with Natalie? She and Ava had a feud. I need to discover what happened. Where it happened. Oh, Serena, the answer is right in front of you. Think!* She stared at the ceiling, hoping for inspiration. *I've got it! Enrique, the dresser.*

"Knock, knock," Jack said, standing in the entryway.

"Jack, come in. I need your help." Serena pointed to the door. "Please close it."

"Okay, take a deep breath and start from the beginning," Jack said, sitting on her peach sofa.

Serena longed to snuggle against him but remained in her computer chair. She retold the events of the day, staying factual. "Ruby's story gave me a clue to Natalie's motive." She covered her face with her hands. "Oh, Jack, I like Natalie, but I think she did it."

"Hey." Jack's hands grasped onto hers and gently took them away from her face. "Come here."

Serena rose from her seat and fell into his arms. His body warmth soothed her, and she stayed in his embrace until she calmed. "Jack." Serena drew back and met his eyes. "What do you think?"

"I think I need to speak with Enrique."

"Can *we* speak with him?"

Jack narrowed his eyes. "If I say no, will Nina call me?"

"Probably." Serena pressed her lips together.

"Fine." Jack huffed.

"Is he available?" Serena asked. "Or did Enrique leave with the others on Monday?"

"No, he never checked out with me."

"I know why," Serena said, and gave Jack a smile. "He accepted Mia's gift. Enrique is still in the hotel."

"Then, here's the plan. Start with Mia. Let her contact him and explain why we need him. I'm going to the station and will bring Jonathan here."

"Why Jonathan?"

"Jonathan and Natalie must be in the same room. No more lies. One can't blame the other."

"I like it." Serena nodded. "Will Detective Mitchell release Teddy? He should come, too."

"I doubt it, Serena. He's a stubborn man and will need concrete proof before he does."

"Okay," Serena said. "Let's get started. I've only got till midnight."

Jack pulled his brows together. "What happens at midnight?"

"I turn into a pumpkin."

"I highly doubt you could turn into a pumpkin." Jack gave her a quick kiss and started for the door.

"Jack, wait." Serena approached him. "Where should we meet? The bar is not available, and we need somewhere private."

After a long pause, Jack said, "The bridal room. It might also be the scene of the crime."

Serena checked her watch. "It's almost dinnertime. Make sure you eat something to keep up your energy." She giggled. "Sorry, I went into mom mode."

"I didn't take it that way. It showed me you cared." Jack captured her lips in a hot, searing kiss. "See you later."

✳ ✳ ✳ ✳

Serena quickened her pace the closer she got to the tearoom. She promised Jack she'd eat, but her stomach said otherwise. *I can handle a cup of tea and a scone.* Flying past the pond, Sam poked his head out of the water, appearing to encourage Serena on her quest. "Sam, you were right," she called. "Teddy is innocent."

Lily and Mia met her at the door, anxious expressions on their faces.

"You did it, Serena," Mia said, taking her hand and guiding her to their table. "What's the next step?"

Serena told about her meeting with Ruby. "After she left, it came to me. Enrique may hold the answers we need."

Before Serena could ask her, Mia said, "Where do you want me to bring him?"

"We chose the bridal room."

"I'll send someone to unlock it and prepare the room for company," Nina said, standing behind Mia.

"Grandmother," Mia said, holding her hand over her heart. "You always come out of nowhere."

"Thank you, my dear." Nina smiled. "Anything else I can do?"

"We'll let you know," Mia said.

Nina dipped her head and walked to a nearby table.

"That woman is remarkable." Serena chuckled.

"What about me?" Lily asked. "I want to help."

"You're in charge of Natalie," Serena said. "If she sees me, she may suspect something. We already said our goodbyes."

"Say I sent you," Mia told Lily. "I offered the Takeda jet to fly her home."

"Okay, I'll tell her it's ready, and I'm supposed to escort her to the limo. Here's the tricky part. How do I direct her to the bridal room instead?"

"We need to time this precisely," Serena replied. "When I hear from Jack, the plan goes into motion. You will get the P.I.C. message, which means, 'It's a go.' I'll wait in the bridal room in case anyone arrives early. Mia invites Enrique to join her there, and you'll escort Natalie to the lobby."

"That's when I intervene," Nina said.

"Grandmother!" Mia jumped. "Stop! My heart."

"Sorry, granddaughter, in our field of work, you must learn to always expect surprises."

Serena wrinkled her brow. *Their field of work? Hotel ownership and the fashion world? I guess so?* "What will you say, Nina?" she asked.

"Leave that up to me, Serena," Nina answered. "Lily and I will handle Ms. Grey."

"I'm sure you will." Serena smiled and looked at the people surrounding her. "A year ago, you weren't part of my world." She blinked back tears. "Now you're a huge part of it. You've supported me when I wrote my book, helped me clear my name and haven't stopped me from discovering who killed Ava."

"We have the same likes and ideas which bonded us. Plus, we're strong women and no one tells us what to do," Lily said. She paused as she glanced around the table. "Except for Nina."

As the women shared a laugh, Serena's gaze shifted to Nina, only to find she had vanished.

* * * *

"This has to work." Serena inspected the area, searching for clues the police may have overlooked.

Serena walked to the ornamental fireplace surrounded by seating. *We can use this area for our interrogation.* She kept checking her phone, but it remained silent. "What if Bill is preventing Jack from taking Jonathan from the station? This is a job for Super Nina." Sitting in one of the comfortable leather chairs, she called her.

"Serena, has something happened?"

"No, but I'm worried. Bill Mitchell may challenge Jack's decision to bring Jonathan to The Pearl. He believes he caught the killer, Ted Lewis, so why not release Jonathan?" Serena huffed. "He just wants to impress his boss."

"The commissioner?"

"Yep, Jack said he's a friend of yours."

"More of an acquaintance. I see Daniel at charity functions. We are on friendly terms."

"Could you speak with Daniel? Tell him it is vital to the investigation to release Jonathan in Jack's care. Jack would never involve you or use the Takeda name, so I'm doing it for him."

"Very loyal, Serena. I'll contact Daniel as soon as we end this call."

Serena sent air kisses, although Nina could not see her. "Thank you."

A half hour had passed before she heard from Jack. "Finally leaving the station with Jonathan."

Doing a happy dance in her head, Serena sent the P.I.C. message to Lily and Mia. "It's on!" Her heart pounded, not knowing what to expect. "Should I sit or stand? Sit, like I belonged here."

Serena face-timed the girls and her mom while she waited. They peppered her with questions, and she told them she couldn't divulge confidential information until the investigation ended. She promised to come home tomorrow morning and provide answers. A noise came at the door, so she finished their conversation with, "I love you."

"Why are we coming in here?" Jonathan asked.

"Because I said so," Jack said in a gravelly voice.

"Serena?" Jonathan raised his brows and dropped his jaw. "What are you doing here?"

"Same thing as Jack. Solving this crime."

"Sit." Jack pointed to a chair in front of a vanity, unlocked one of Jonathan's handcuffs and attached it to the chair.

"Really?" Jonathan pulled on the chain fastened to the chair. "This little thing won't keep me from escaping…not that I plan to run."

"If you do, you'll drag the little thing with you," Jack snarled. He turned to Serena. "I didn't think I'd get out of the station. I argued with Bill for an hour. He insisted I fill out paperwork which had nothing to do with the case. When I handed in the forms, he gave the okay to leave." Jack snapped his fingers. "Just like that. No debate. Nothing."

"You got through to him, Jack. Good job," Serena replied. "It's all set. Everyone should be on their way."

"What's going on here?" Jonathan yelled. "I demand to know. I have rights."

"Truthfully?" Serena asked, lifting a brow. "We're waiting for Natalie to join us."

The door burst open, and Lily, Nina and Natalie walked into the room. Natalie didn't quite walk, it appeared Lily had a tight grip on her arm and pulled her inside.

"No! I don't have to go with you," Natalie cried.

"Natalie," Nina said. "Things will go easier if you calm down."

"Calm down?" Natalie yanked her arm from Lily's hand. "Fine. What do you want?"

"I'd like you to sit over there," Jack said, gesturing to the leather furniture grouping where Serena sat. "We're waiting on one more guest."

Mia and Enrique entered the bridal room within minutes of the last group. When Enrique spotted Jack, he raised his hands and shook them. "No, no, no. You've already cleared me of any wrongdoing."

"Enrique," Mia said. "I keep telling you, it's okay. You did nothing wrong. I want you to retell what happened between Ava and Natalie."

"Whatever he says, it's a lie," Natalie said in a teary voice.

"Let him speak." Jack bobbed his head toward the man.

Enrique cleared his throat. "I have worked with many finicky models but none so much as this one." He gestured at Natalie. "She insisted on dressing alone behind the curtain. When she'd step out, I could barely touch her to adjust the outfit."

"Why is that, Natalie?" Jack asked.

"I don't like to be touched."

"I can vouch for that," Serena said, recalling the times she tried to hug her.

Mia gave Natalie a strange look. "If that's true, why did you choose to model? Dressers, make-up artists and people assisting you to the stage must touch you."

"I'll get over it," Natalie replied. "I promise."

Chapter Twenty One

"I gathered you here," Jack declared. "So Enrique can describe what happened between Natalie and Ava. Natalie and Jonathan, it seems you are shielding each other, but my intention is to uncover the truth. You're both present, so no passing responsibility to someone else." He faced Enrique. "If you would please."

"I will try my best," Enrique said. "Natalie approached me and politely asked permission to dress herself. I, of course, could not believe she asked. When I explained the inner workings of a dressing room, she argued with me. Instead of fighting, I let Natalie go into the dressing area alone. It was her first show, and I assumed she still had to learn protocol." He looked at Mia. "I planned to speak with you after the show."

Mia nodded. "It's okay. You did nothing wrong. Go on with your story."

"Ava overheard the conversation and took it upon herself to correct the young woman. She called Natalie names I will not repeat. Natalie yelled at Ava and told her to never speak to her again. It ended quickly. Ava flipped her hair over her shoulder and stormed away. I was grateful it was over."

"Thank you, Enrique," Jack said. "It wasn't enough reason to kill Ava, was it, Natalie?"

"No." Natalie shook her head and gazed at the floor.

"So, what was it?" Serena asked. "There's another reason."

"Nothing. That's it." Natalie pointed at Jonathan. "What about him? He served her the champagne."

"I delivered it to the door," Jonathan protested. "I'm not allowed inside."

"According to Jonathan's statement," Jack said. "He delivered an empty glass and full champagne bottle to the door. Is that correct?"

"Yes." Jonathan dipped his head.

"Who took the tray from you?"

"A model."

"Did you recognize her?"

"No, I swear."

Jack held up his pointer finger. "The empty glass is the key. Wouldn't someone notice a liquid or powder in an empty champagne flute?"

A shiver went through Serena, and she rubbed her arms. The touching sensation brought back a memory. Natalie had walked up to the bar, distraught, and Serena reached out to comfort her. She'd given the woman a light hug before she pulled away.

"Natalie, stand up," she demanded.

"Why?"

Serena met Jack's eyes and hoped he got the message. *Trust me. I figured it out.*

"Natalie," Jack said in a stern tone.

"Fine." Natalie stood in place.

Serena studied the outfit Natalie wore. She had on a long-sleeve denim shirt dress that buttoned down the front. The hem ended above her knees. *I can do this.*

After inhaling deeply and slowly exhaling, Serena approached the woman. Placing her hands on either side of the open collar, she gave a strong tug. Buttons popped from the dress, spilling onto the floor.

"What are you doing?" Natalie screamed.

"Exposing you, in more ways than one," Serena answered and stepped away from her.

A collective gasp filled the room, then silence.

"This is why she didn't want anyone to hug or touch her. It's the reason she wouldn't let Enrique dress her. Natalie wanted to become a plus-size model so she could break into the fashion world. To her, it was the easiest way. For over a year, she's tried to gain weight, but I have a feeling she didn't reach her goal." Serena pointed to the padded suit Natalie wore under her dress. "This helped."

"Clever," Jonathan said.

"Shut up, Jonathan," Natalie screamed. "What does this prove? I cheated so Mia would hire me. Lock me up."

"No," Serena replied. "As I listened to Enrique's story, I put the pieces together. How close did Ava get to you, Natalie? Did she see the suit?"

Tears flowed down Natalie's cheeks. "Okay, yes. She used it as leverage against me. Ava threatened to expose me and taunted me every chance she got. It became unbearable. The night before the show, I bought some sleeping pills on the street. After I saw her pour the champagne, I emptied the capsules into her drink. I didn't mean for her to die. I wanted Ava to appear drunk and unstable on the runway. I hoped if she tried to reveal the truth, no one would believe her." She pulled her dress around her body. "I think I need a lawyer." She put her head in her hands and sobbed. "I didn't mean for her to die."

"I have one more question," Jack said. "Did you sabotage the shoes?"

"Yes," Natalie said through tears.

"Why?"

"Stella and Aurora deserved it, so I used them as test subjects. If the heel broke, then Ava's shoe would do the same."

"How did you get their codes?" Enrique cried.

"It wasn't hard." Natalie smirked. "No one seemed to notice me. It gave me an advantage. Plus, I have a good memory."

"No need to say more," Serena stated calmly. "Is it enough?" She looked at Jack.

Serena listened as he read Natalie her rights, and her heart plunged to her stomach. A sickening sensation inside her continued to intensify, despite having resolved the case. She wanted to sit next to Natalie and cry along with her.

Nina's arm slipped around Serena's waist. "Let's go for a walk." She guided Serena out the door and headed for the gardens. "It's your first case. You thought you would feel elated."

"Yes," Serena mumbled. "Don't get me wrong. I'm glad we caught the actual person, and Ted Lewis can go free. It's not what I expected, that's all."

"It will get better," Nina said.

"I'm not planning on solving another crime, Nina." Serena gave her a sad smile.

"Never say never," Nina uttered, pausing by the pond. "I'll leave you here."

The fountain, the focal point of the pond, provided a source of relaxation. The sound of trickling and splashing water distracted Serena from the range of emotions she felt. When a red-faced koi appeared, tears filled her eyes. "I didn't expect it to be her, Sam," she whispered.

Sam looked at Serena with soulful eyes, appearing to understand. "I take pride in my ability to judge people's character. Think of the customers I chauffeured around town. I could always sense if their good side outweighed the bad, especially when it came to tipping. It proved me right every time," she joked. "I hope I still can read people."

The fish seemed to nod, or Serena thought so. "I hope they let Teddy free tonight. He doesn't deserve another night behind bars. We believed in him, Sam. Hey." Serena pointed to the koi. "Is it okay for Jonathan and me to become friends?"

Serena already knew the answer. "Yes." She laughed at the expression on Sam's face when he popped out of the water. "That helps." Her phone buzzed. "Hang on. It's Jack." She read his message. "He's taking Natalie to the station but wants me to wait for him." She answered him by typing, "I'll be in the bar."

* * * *

Sitting at a table close to the entrance, Serena nursed a glass of white wine. She felt the need to order something, but drinking didn't appeal to her. Her heart had taken a beating and still raced when she replayed the earlier events in her mind. It wouldn't stop until she took deep, calming breaths.

"Is this seat taken?"

Jack's voice brought tears to her eyes. "I'm saving it for you."

"Hey." Jack gripped her hand. "You're crying."

"Nina said the first one is the hardest."

"The first one?"

"That's what I thought. Does she think it could happen again?" Serena asked through her tears. "I've had enough drama for the year." She sniffed. "Did you deliver Natalie to the police?"

"I did." Jack nodded. "I have something that might help you feel better." He waved to a person waiting in the shadows.

"Serena?" Teddy appeared before her.

"Teddy!" Serena jumped from her chair into his open arms. "It's good to see you."

"Same here." Teddy chuckled. "Thanks for not giving up on me."

"Please join us," Serena said, returning to her seat.

"Thanks for the offer, but Jack booked a room for me. I'm going to shower, shave and change." Teddy shook his head. "What a shame about Natalie. I saw the talent in her." He patted Serena's shoulder. "Thanks, friend. I hope we meet again under better circumstances."

"Now I'm really going to cry." Serena wiped her eyes. "You stay in touch. Don't disappear from my life."

Teddy bobbed his head once and headed for the exit.

"You believed in him, Serena, and never wavered," Jack said.

"Oh, I wavered." Serena's laugh had a hollow ring to it. "You did it, Jack. You solved the case."

"Let's get out of here," Jack suggested, ignoring her comment. "I owe you a walk in the garden."

Serena liked the idea. "And I want you to meet someone."

Jack took Serena's hand and helped her from her chair. Not once did he release his grip, even when they reached the pond. "Do you want to sit?" he asked.

"Yes, but first let's watch the fish." Serena tugged on his hand. When she got to the railing, she called, "Sam? Samurai?"

The koi leisurely glided by, but no red fish burst from the water eager to see her. She studied the water, trying to find him.

"Who's Sam or Samurai?" Jack asked.

"A friend." Serena shook her head. "One of the koi. He's beautiful. Red body, white fins and tail with a white underbelly."

"He might be busy with the ladies," Jack teased. "Or sleeping. It's almost midnight."

Confused, Serena gave up the search for Sam. "Let's sit."

"I've got something for you," Jack said, fumbling in his jacket pocket before he pulled out a small, rectangular black box. He placed it in Serena's hand.

"What? When did you do this?"

"I make time for you, Serena."

Not wanting to burst into tears again, Serena concentrated on the box. She lifted the lid and gasped. A glass slipper, no more than three inches, shimmered under the lights. A ruby red gem shaped like a heart adorned the top of the shoe.

Jack pointed to the heart. "Your birthstone. July, right?"

"How did you…" Serena chuckled. "Never mind. You have ways of discovering any information you need. I love it."

"You'll never turn into a pumpkin," Jack said. "This is a reminder."

Serena waved her hand in front of her face. "Stop. I've cried enough for one day." She gazed down at the slipper. "It's beautiful and thoughtful, Jack." She placed her hand on his cheek. "Thank you."

"No, thank you. I was going through life, not really seeing it, until I met you. You changed me, Serena. It's only been a short while, and as we mentioned earlier, we want to take it slow. But you're the person who was missing from my life. I want to see where this goes."

"I feel the same," Serena whispered.

"On that note, what are you doing this weekend?"

* * * *

Serena woke the next morning feeling refreshed and ready to take on the world. She messaged her family she'd be home in a few hours and got ready for the day. After dressing in a casual blue sweater and black jeans, her phone pinged. "Mia?" She read, "Meet me for breakfast in the restaurant. I know you want to get home, so I won't keep you." Serena giggled and answered back, "Aren't you sick of me by now?" In return, she received, "Never."

Breakfast with a friend sounded like the cure she needed. No agenda. No secret meetings. Serena packed up her belongings and called the front desk. "I'm checking out. Is it possible to hold my bags until I'm ready to leave?"

"Yes, we can, Ms. Tate, but you don't need to check out."

"Won't someone need the room?"

"No," the clerk said. "It's your room."

"Mine?" Serena glanced around the two-room suite. "No, there must be a mistake."

"If you'd like to speak with the manager…"

"No, I'll go higher than that," Serena answered and ended the call.

Nina answered on the first ring, as always. "Hello, Serena. I hope you had a good night's sleep."

"I did, but that's not why I'm calling. It's too much. A free office and now a free room?"

"A lifetime free room," Nina corrected her. "You are one of us, Serena. A granddaughter of my heart. Although." She chuckled. "More like a daughter. I'm not that old."

"I'll take either," Serena said in a lighthearted voice. "But really I can't accept…"

"You can, and you will."

What did Lily say? We're strong women and don't need to listen to anyone, except Nina. "I'll accept your generous offer. I don't know how I'll ever repay you."

"One day I may need you, Serena. When the time arrives, it will be thanks enough."

Serena's heart raced. "Are you expecting something to happen?"

"My goodness, no. Enjoy your breakfast."

She knows everything! "I will. Then I'm taking a short break from work to plan the girls' eighteenth birthday."

"That sounds wonderful."

"You're invited, of course."

"As I said, it sounds wonderful."

"Okay, I get it. A bunch of teens going crazy at a party doesn't sound appealing."

"I'll send a gift. Take care, Serena."

"Nina? She hung up." Serena shook her head and smiled. "Such an interesting yet complex woman. I love her." She checked through her rooms one more time. "What am I doing? If I forgot something, it will be here."

Grabbing her handbag and jacket, Serena opened the door, took a quick look at her new home away from home, and headed for breakfast. As she walked toward the table, Serena blinked back tears.

"Surprise!" Lily said, waving her hands.

Teddy sat to one side of Lily, Mia on the other. Teddy rose from his chair and helped Serena to her seat. "Good morning."

"Teddy," Serena whispered. "You look like you haven't slept."

"I haven't." Teddy smiled. "This time it was for a valid reason." He presented her with a shopping bag with handles. "For you."

"You went shopping instead of sleeping?" Serena asked.

"Serena, open your present," Mia said. "It will answer all your questions."

Serena noticed an absence of place settings, and on closer inspection, no one had any coffee or tea. "What's going on?"

"Let me." Teddy reached into the bag and put two black leather albums in front of her. He rested his hand on top of one. "This is Jade's portfolio. Some agents want to see a book, but most prefer online portfolios. I've made the girls both. Also, I left a few blank pages for more poses. I never had time to finish."

"Teddy." Serena touched her throat. "I don't know what to say."

"Say nothing. I can never repay what you've done for me." Teddy flipped open the book and pointed as he went along. "Headshot. Full-length shot. Editorial Fashion Shot. Smiling."

Astonished, Serena asked. "You did all this with the girls?"

"Sorry, I couldn't do more. I planned to work with them after the show." Teddy switched Jade's book with Jewel's. "Same categories as Jade's book. The camera loves your girls."

"They'll be thrilled, Teddy. Why don't you come to their party and present them with the books."

"A party filled with teenagers and raging hormones?" Teddy teased. "Sorry. Been there. Done that."

"It will be the best present ever," Serena replied. "The girls will love it."

"There's more," Mia said.

"I don't know if my heart can take it." Serena placed a hand on her chest.

"A book for you, Serena." Teddy handed Lily and Mia the portfolios, and they dove into the books.

Teddy had included some identical photos, but as Serena flipped to another page, she gasped. He'd posed the girls back-to-back, glancing over their shoulders at the camera. They sported those familiar little girl smiles they'd flash at her when plotting something she wouldn't like. She kept turning the pages, exclaiming over the photos.

"These are all eight by tens, Serena," Teddy said. "You don't need to leave the photos in the book. Pull any out for framing. If you want a different size, let me know."

Love and joy filled Serena until she felt she could burst. "Don't you dare leave my life, Theodore Lewis. You're stuck with me."

"Point taken." Teddy smiled.

"Will you two stop?" Lily lifted her glasses and dabbed her eyes with a tissue. "I can't take anymore." She leaned forward and grinned. "Not really. Keep going."

"I think we're finished, right, Teddy?" Serena asked.

"Great," Mia said. "How about some breakfast?"

Chapter Twenty Two

During the weeks leading up to the twins' birthday, Serena found a steady rhythm to her days. She commuted to her office, dedicating time to her latest novel while the girls were in school. She'd come home to help with homework and birthday preparations. Jack took her on weekend dates, visited the house when he could, and even ate dinner with the family. The girls approved and invited him to their birthday.

Serena gave in and purchased a karaoke machine for the party, but it got a workout before the big day. Not only did the girls try it out, but Serena also found her mom in the basement, singing her heart out. That day she sneaked down the stairs and videoed the act for the girls. When her mom had spotted her, Robin chased Serena through the house, wanting her to delete the footage. Serena promised she would after the girls had seen it. She reveled in the normalcy and wondered how long it would last.

The day of the party, Mia arrived early. "I can't stay, Serena. Kade and I are taking a needed vacation. We leave this afternoon."

"Sounds wonderful. Where are you going?"

"Hawaii."

Serena hugged her friend. "Have a great time. Eat pineapple and drink Mai Tais and pina coladas. Forget about the real world and indulge."

"We plan to, although Kade will drink margaritas." Mia giggled. "Are the girls here?"

"In the basement, putting up the final decorations." Serena went to the steps. "Jade, Jewel? Mia is here."

The pounding on the stairs showed they'd heard and couldn't wait to see her. "Mia, did you see our portfolios?" Jade asked.

"I certainly did. Very professional. As a matter of fact." Mia tapped the side of her mouth and looked at the ceiling. "It made me want to hire you."

While the girls celebrated, Serena widened her eyes and whispered, "Mia."

"You'll approve, Serena," Mia answered.

"For a show? When is it?" Jewel asked after she and Jade stopped bouncing.

"This summer, I haven't set the date yet. It's a charity event in honor of Ava Taylor. The money raised will go into a scholarship fund for kids who are talented but can't afford fine arts high schools and liberal arts colleges."

"You turned a tragedy into a positive, Mia," Serena said. "Kudos. The girls don't need my permission, but I am all for it."

"We'll be out of school, too," Jewel said. "And can concentrate only on modeling."

"Until you go to college," Serena reminded her.

"I really must go," Mia said. "Happy birthday, Jade and Jewel. I hope you like my present."

"Like?" Jade exclaimed. "It's the best."

Serena walked Mia to the door. "They're thrilled. Between you and Teddy, I guess my karaoke machine pales in comparison."

"Nonsense. They're gifts." Mia kissed Serena's cheek. "Enjoy. I'll see you in two weeks."

"Hello," Justice said as Serena opened the front door. "It's good to see you again, Ms. Takeda."

"Please call me Mia." Mia waved to Serena and rolled her eyes. "Good luck."

"Come in, Justice. The girls are in the basement. Chaperones in the kitchen."

"Should I act as a guest or chaperone?" Justice teased.

"Whatever you'd like," Serena replied.

Jack's car pulled into the drive, and Serena's stomach flipped as it always did. "Go in, Justice. Mom will put you to work."

"Isn't that the security guard from The Pearl?" Justice asked, narrowing his eyes.

"He's also a detective on the police force, Justice."

"Not from what I found."

"You stalked him?" Serena folded her arms.

Employed at a software company, Justice was hired for his excellent computer skills. Serena pictured him diligently searching for information about Jack, hoping to find some incriminating evidence.

"No." Justice shook his head. "I never believed he was a detective. I did a little search in my spare time. Jack Ando works full-time for The Pearl…as a security guard."

From the corner of her eye, Serena saw Jack open his car door. "Could you please go inside, Justice?"

"I thought you should know." Justice lifted his shoulder. "What else could he lie about?"

Serena pushed him into the house and let the screen door go. She hadn't believed a word he'd said.

"Serena?" Jack trotted across the grass to reach her. "You okay?"

"I'm fine. It's Justice being Justice."

"What did he say?"

"It doesn't matter," Serena answered.

"From the look on your face, it does."

Two cars pulled into the driveway, and Serena noticed parents in the driver's seats. *I like it. Obeying the rules. Teens can't drive other teens their first year of driving.* Eight kids emerged and headed toward the house.

"Hey, everyone," Serena said, recognizing them from school events or visits to the house. "Party is in the basement."

After counting twenty guests, the stream of traffic slowed, and Serena faced Jack. "It's stupid, Jack. Justice said you don't work for the police department."

"He's right. I don't."

"No-o-o."

"Let's back up. I worked at the department until the day I wanted to bring Jonathan to The Pearl. Bill and I argued for over two hours. Finally, he offered me a deal. He'd release Jonathan if I resigned from the force."

Stunned, Serena remembered calling Nina for help. *Was I too late? Nina would never agree to this.*

"If you recall, I said I had paperwork to complete unrelated to the case. I was working on those and my resignation letter."

"Why?"

"Solving the case and charging the correct person was more important than my job. Besides, I didn't enjoy working with Bill. He's pig-headed."

Serena giggled. "True."

"If Justice recently looked into my work history, all he'd see on my work history is security guard."

"That's how you like it," Serena said.

Over the past weeks, Jack had confided he'd been Special Opps in the service and worked undercover for years at the L.A.P.D. Nina only hired the best. "I'll never know when I'll need your skills," she had told them.

"Yes, Serena, I have my secrets, but now you know them." Jack put his arm around her waist and pulled her to him. "Let Justice believe what he wants. It's better that way."

"I'm calling Nina tomorrow. She'll get you reinstated."

"No." Jack kissed her mouth. "You won't." He kissed her again. "It gives me more time with you."

Serena placed her hands on his cheeks. "Jack Ando, you're one hell of a man."

"And you, Serena Tate, are a force to be reckoned with. I can't wait to see where life takes us next."

"Mom! Are you coming in?" Jewel called. "We're starting karaoke."

"Yes, Jack and I have picked the perfect song," Serena answered.

Jack lifted his brow. "We have?"

"Oh, yes, we have." Serena took advantage of their moment alone and kissed him with a passion she hoped he felt, too.

Jack responded to the kiss, pulling her closer and whispering, "Whatever the song is, I don't care. As long as I sing it with you."

The End

Before You Go

Join Nancy's Mailing List and never miss a release!
Nancypennick.com

THANK YOU FOR READING

Did you enjoy this book?
I invite you to leave a review at your favorite book site,
such as Goodreads, BookBub and Amazon.

DID YOU KNOW THAT LEAVING A REVIEW…

Helps other readers find books they may enjoy.
Gives you a chance to let your voice be heard.
Gives authors recognition for their hard work.
Doesn't have to be long. A sentence or two about why
you liked the book will do.

Other Books by Nancy Pennick

The $ecret Billionaire $ociety
(Contemporary Romantic Suspense)

<u>*Chase (Book 1)*</u>
<u>*Nash (Book 2)*</u>
<u>*Finn (Book 3)*</u>
<u>*Beau (Book 4)*</u>
<u>*Gabe (Book 5)*</u>
<u>*Kade (Book 6)*</u>
<u>*The Elusive Mr. Smith (Book 7)*</u>
<u>*Smith's Revenge (Book 8)*</u>

The Billionaire's Bride
(Contemporary Romantic Suspense Series)

<u>*Vanessa (Book 1)*</u>
<u>*Grace (Book 2)*</u>
<u>*Charlotte (Book 3)*</u>
<u>*Tess (Book 4)*</u>
<u>*Lily (Book 5)*</u>
<u>*Mia (Book 6)*</u>

The Clan MacLaren Series
(Historical Romance)

My Highlander Husband (Book 1)
Donnach's Daughter (Book 2)
The Heart of the Emerald (Book 3)
Now and Forever (Book 4)
MacLaren Strong (Book 5)
Homecoming (Book 6)

ABOUT THE AUTHOR

For three decades, Nancy taught elementary school. She'd written short stories as a child, kept a diary and loved the writing process. After retiring, she hadn't set out to become an author, but when inspiration struck, she couldn't resist putting pen to paper. She now had time to follow her dream. Today her writing spans various genres, including young adult, historical romance, romantic suspense and cozy mysteries.

Nancy lives with her husband, Ron, and has a married son, who helps her with tech more than he likes! Plus, add in a wonderful daughter-in-law and grandson which makes her life complete.